BELIEVING IN YOU

THE SAN DIEGO MARINES SERIES, BOOK FOUR

JESS MASTORAKOS

To get a free copy of the prequel, Forever with You, visit: http://jessmastorakos.com/forever-with-you

1

IVY

"You did what?" I asked, my hand trembling as I set down the mug of coffee I'd just poured.

"We already set up your profile," Rachel said. She cast a glance at Nora, then looked back at me. "Don't hate us."

I crossed my arms over my chest. "Oh, too late. I completely hate you."

"Ivy," Nora smiled like the Cheshire cat. "We knew you wouldn't do it yourself. So we took care of it."

"Maybe I wouldn't do it myself because I didn't want it done." I threw my hands up in frustration. I could feel my cheeks getting red as realization dawned on me. "Wait, when did you do this? Is it too late to take it down before anyone sees it?"

Nora and Rachel exchanged a guilty look, and Nora

shrugged. "The wine was flowing. I honestly don't know what time we finished it. Late last night."

My hands twitched out in their direction. "Let me see it, maybe it's not too late."

Rachel crinkled her nose. "I'm sorry, Vee. My phone is still logged into it, and I've been getting blown up all morning. Or, I guess, you have."

My eyes bulged nearly out of their sockets. "What?"

Rachel took her phone out of the pocket of her workout leggings—her uniform as our school's PE teacher—and opened it to the dating app. "Holy crap, you have seventeen Connection Requests."

"What does that mean?" I snatched the phone out of her hands and tried to make sense of what I was seeing. I'd never signed up for a dating app before and had no idea how to navigate the platform. Sure enough, however, I could tell that whatever a Connection Request was, I had seventeen of them. My stomach turned as I realized that these were all living, breathing men, weighing in on the profile that I hadn't even set up for myself.

Nora looked concerned. "Are you okay?"

I glared up at her. "I'm not sure yet."

Rachel picked up my World's Best Teacher coffee mug from the counter behind me and brought it to the table Nora was sitting at. She pulled out a chair and gestured to it. "Sit. Let's have a look at these Connection Requests. Lunch is almost over."

I closed my eyes, sighed deeply, then lowered myself into the chair. "Why did you guys think this would be a good idea? When you asked me if I'd ever consider dating again, I had no idea saying 'yes' meant ... this."

"Vee, you just seem so sad all the time," Rachel said, giving me a small, pitying smile. "I know you were with Cory since ... well, forever. So that's understandable. But still, it wouldn't kill you to get back out there."

Nora nodded. "Agreed."

I shot Nora an accusatory look. "You won't even text that cute guy you met last weekend."

"I'm waiting for him to text me," she replied.

"Mm-hmm." I turned to Rachel. "And you only see your boyfriend at the gym."

"We're both really busy," Rachel defended herself. "And our love lives aren't the issue here. Yours is. You need a rebound."

I bit my lip. I'd never liked the idea of a rebound. What, that's the person you date right after someone you loved, and you're supposed to use them to get over your ex? How is that fair to the rebound? It's not.

"The thing is, I feel like Cory led me on. Like, here I was expecting him to propose, and he dumps me instead. I was blindsided. I don't want to lead someone else on just so I can get over my issues. It doesn't feel right."

Rachel reached out and put a hand on my knee. "You don't have to lead someone on. You can have fun conversations or go on a really great date. You don't have to promise them this big commitment. Just ... I don't know ...."

"Find a super-hot guy, and have a little fun to get out of your funk," Nora finished for her.

"Precisely," Rachel said.

I raised my chin to the ceiling and sighed. "I'm not going to win this, am I?"

They both shook their heads and laughed, causing another sigh to escape me. I handed the phone back to Rachel. "You'll need to show me how to work this app. I have no idea what I'm doing."

"On it," Nora said, rubbing her hands together with a devilish smile.

For the rest of our lunch break, my two best friends schooled me on Connect, America's current favorite dating app. I learned that a Connection Request was where a user sees a profile they like and basically "favorite" it. Seventeen guys had Favorited me. If I Like them back, a Connection is made and we're able to start messaging. If I don't, I hit Ignore and they'll never know.

Once I knew my way around the app, it was time to

check out the guys who had requested me. Bachelor number one was cute, or at least his picture was. My friends weren't sensitive to my fears of being catfished. According to my friends, it's a necessary risk with online dating, and if you let that get into your head, you wouldn't have a very good time. After seeing that he was a pediatrician—and hearing my girlfriends swoon over how cute he was for choosing to work with kids—I made the Connection. And on we went, nixing the guys who looked like weirdos and making Connections with the cute ones who had stable jobs. By the end of our lunch hour, we'd made our way through all of the pending Connection Requests and even sent out a few of our own. I had to admit, it was actually kind of fun.

That is, until a message came through and I about jumped out of my skin. "What do I do?"

Nora rolled her eyes as she gathered up her bag to head back to class. "We don't have time to deal with it now, so we'll check it out when we get home."

"Besides," Rachel added, handing me back my phone after installing the app on it instead of keeping my profile logged in on hers, "you don't want to seem too eager. He can wait a few hours. Where's the fire?"

I narrowed my eyes at her. "Really?"

"Oops," she said, making an awkward face as she remembered my ex was a firefighter. "I'll skip the fire jokes."

Without another word, I turned on my heel and headed toward my classroom. Online dating. Me. The girl who'd been in love with the same guy since elementary school. The girl who'd thought she'd one day marry that guy and skip out on the awkwardness of dating altogether. Not for the first time that day, I silently cursed Cory Roberts and his big-city dreams. This was all his fault.

A s was custom on a Friday night after work, the three of us girls stopped at the grocery store on our way home. We grabbed some wine, snacks, and ingredients for Saturday morning brunch.

By the time we pulled up to the cute bungalow we shared in the trendiest neighborhood in Fort Worth, Nora and Rachel had worn themselves out trying to get me excited to answer my Connect messages. They had no way to understand how I felt about it. Both of them had experienced dating since we were teenagers. They weren't scared to put themselves out there with someone new. Fear of rejection was something they'd gotten used to in the dating world. But in my case, my first taste of rejection had come when my boyfriend of eleven years dumped me and moved away. Forgive me for being nervous about putting my heart out there again.

Once we were settled with our wine and snacks, we hopped back on the app. My stomach turned with anxiety over what I'd find in my inbox. To my utter shock, I had seven messages. Which meant that all seven of the Connections I'd made earlier in the day had resulted in a message from each guy I'd Favorited.

My eyes flew from the screen to my friends. "Ugh. I don't know if I can do this. There's seven messages. I have to juggle seven guys at once?"

Nora chuckled. "I mean, you're not dating all seven of them."

"Everyone kind of figures that you're talking to other people on the app," Rachel explained.

Nora held up a finger. "That is, until you have that whole exclusivity conversation. Which usually means you both delete the app altogether."

I gulped.

Rachel took a sip of her wine and waved a hand. "Let's not worry about that yet. Just start with the first message."

I nodded and tapped the first message in my inbox, waiting for it to load. It was from the pediatrician. I cleared my throat and read the message to my friends.

Mark: Hey, teacher. I have to say, after being in school for so many years to become a doctor, I was

hesitant to reach out to you. But if you're really as beautiful as your picture suggests, you're worth it.

Rachel made a gagging noise, and Nora scrunched her face in disgust.

"I guess we're not fans of Mark?" I asked with a chuckle.

Nora shook her head. "We already knew he was a doctor from his profile. Why did he need to be so braggy in his message? Next."

"Do I ignore it or do I reply and tell him I'm not interested?" I asked, feeling bad for rejecting him even though I was the one who was afraid of being rejected.

"Ignore it." Both of my friends respond at once.

I move to the next message in the inbox. I tell my friends that it's from Chris, an accountant, and read them his message.

Chris: Hey, baby.

"That's it?" Rachel asked.

"Yep," I replied.

Nora shrugs. "I mean, do you like being called 'baby' by someone you don't know?"

"No?" I responded, but it comes out more like a question.

"I say ignore it," Rachel said. "I don't know why he couldn't come up with something more interesting to say."

"Maybe because he's an accountant." Nora pops a chip in her mouth with a wink.

I moved to the next message, read it aloud, and then laughed as my friends shot another guy down. And on it went, until we landed on the sixth message in my inbox.

Robby: Hey, I'm Robby. I'm a mechanic. I want to let you know right off the bat that I have a six-year-old son. You won't meet him unless we turn into a serious thing, but if that's a deal breaker, at least you know up front. Anyway, I think you're really pretty, and you probably like kids if you're a kindergarten teacher, so if you want to talk more, let me know.

I couldn't help it. By the time I'd finished reading Robby's message to my friends, I was swooning. I looked up to see their reactions. Nora was holding a chip halfway to her parted lips, an expression like she'd seen a cute puppy on her face. Rachel had her lips pressed into a thin line with her hand over her heart.

"Aw," Rachel said. "Finally! Something we can work with!"

Nora hopped off the couch and came over to where I sat on our crushed velvet vintage armchair. "Let me see him."

I pulled up Robby's picture and laughed as Nora wagged her eyebrows. This guy was a winner in her eyes, anyway. He had sandy-blond hair and the perfect amount of stubble on his square jaw. Our heads bent together and brows furrowed in concentration as we browsed his profile. In addition to being a mechanic and a single father, he was also a book lover who had a passion for cooking.

"I'm *totally* into this one," Nora said, plucking the phone out of my hand and showing Rachel, who agreed. After handing my phone back to me, she rubbed her hands together. "Now we get to reply."

It only took about twenty minutes of joking around and another glass of wine before I finally hit Reply on my message to Robby.

Me: Hey, Robby. Nice to meet you. Your son is definitely not a deal breaker, but thanks for letting me know. You're right, I do love kids. I saw that you love to cook ... is it a deal breaker that my idea of cooking is Kraft Mac & Cheese? Hope not! Talk soon.

"Whew," I said, putting down my empty wine glass. "Online dating is exhausting."

"You better hope that last message in your inbox is a flop," Nora said with a grin. "It took way too long to write back to Robby."

I stuck my tongue out at her and opened the message. I wasn't sure if I wanted it to be a flop or if I wanted it to be good, but when I opened the message, all I felt was underwhelmed.

"What does it say?" Rachel asked, coming closer to look over my shoulder.

"It just says, 'Hey,'" I said for Nora's benefit, who was busy washing out our salsa bowl at the sink.

"Well, that's anticlimactic," Nora said, turning off the water and drying her hands. "But, at least it's an easy reply."

"It is?" I asked.

Rachel shrugged. "Say hey back. Then, I guess, just wait until he replies again."

I harrumphed and typed out the quick reply, hit Send, and then put my phone down with a sigh. "I guess one out of seven ain't bad."

Rachel put a clip on our bag of tortilla chips and put it back in the cabinet. "I feel like one out of seven is pretty typical. Dating is hard."

"Agreed," Nora chimed in. "This was a fun night. I'm excited to see if anything comes of your conversation with Robby."

I took a seat on a barstool at our kitchen island. It had been kind of fun. Stressful and overwhelming at times, but there was something about the way these interactions felt more like a video game than a real dating scenario that took a lot of the pressure off. If it gets weird, all I have to do is delete the app. No harm, no foul.

"Thanks for doing this for me, guys," I told them.

"I'm not sure if I'm actually going to date anyone I meet on here, but for once the idea of dating doesn't make me want to jump off a bridge and get it over with, so that's a win."

Nora gave me a small smile. "We know it sucks about you and Cory, Vee. Trust us, we get it. We've been there since the beginning, since we were all kids. But when Cory said he didn't know who he was without you, I have to ask—did you kind of get what he meant?"

I looked between her and Rachel, who was suddenly very busy straightening up the kitchen. "What do you mean?"

Rachel faced me with a sheepish expression and crossed her arms across her chest. "You were like, what, eight years old when Cory first told you he loved you?"

Nora nodded. "And then you guys officially became boyfriend and girlfriend in middle school. He was constantly around, being friends with Travis. Do you know who you are without him?"

The mention of my older brother had me squirming in my seat. "I'm not sure."

"Well," Rachel said, coming over to place a hand over mine on the counter, "this dating app is a good way to find out. If nothing else, you'll find out what you don't want in a man."

I snorted. "Oh, gee, can't wait."

2

JAKE

"How'd it go?" Brooks asked as I tossed my phone and cover on my rack. He was sprawled out on the rack next to mine, lounging after a long day.

"Good," I replied. "Master Guns said I'm a go to start checking out after we get back. It's starting to feel real."

Brooks sat up and rested his elbows on his knees. "Murphy, you sure you want to do this, man? I never thought you'd hang up your cammies for civilian life so soon. You're gonna miss being a slave like the rest of us. Admit it."

"Bro," I scoffed, blowing hot air into my cupped hands to bring some feeling back into them, "I'll still be working for the government. It's not like I'm ditching my pension."

"Yeah well, as a Department of Defense employee, you'll be doing the same job as me for, like, three times the pay. Plus, you'll get to grow a beard and not go on deployment. If I want to jab at you for your new cushy lifestyle, you better suck it up and take it."

I chuckled. "You got it, man."

"Anyway, I'm pumped you're going to Fort Worth. Every time I go home on leave we'll get to hang out. Plus, you know, if you ever need anything, I've got plenty of people there I can hook you up with."

"Thanks, Brooks," I said, patting my best friend on the arm before launching myself down on my rack. I was too cold and too tired to take off my boots, so I let them hang over the side of the bed.

I was sure I'd prefer Fort Worth winters over the Japanese winter I was dealing with on this deployment. Since our job in the Marines was to load bombs onto F-18s, we were running out onto the flight line—freezing our tails off—from sunup to sundown. We were only a couple weeks into deployment and I was seriously missing my seventy-five-degree days in San Diego at our home base. I wondered idly how hot the summers in Texas would be and if I'd rather be sweating or freezing.

"Plus," Brooks continued, his Southern drawl in full force, "when I get out, the wife and I are moving back home. You know we're both close with family and stuff, so it makes sense. So, I'll see you then, too."

"Dude, you have like twelve years left until retirement."

He sighed, throwing his head back and closing his eyes. "Don't remind me."

Brooks and I were newly promoted sergeants in the Marine Corps, having joined around the same time. We'd each done our first four-year enlistment, come back for a second one, and were nearing the end of that term now. Brooks chose to sign for a third and had his reenlistment ceremony already. I, on the other hand, applied for a job with the Department of Defense at the Naval Air Station Joint Reserve Base in Fort Worth.

I never thought I'd get hired. It was a long shot for sure. But when they'd called me and offered me the gig, I couldn't say no. It was the opportunity to combine my eight years of active duty with twelve years at the DOD to equal a twenty-year career. Which, thankfully, meant I'd still get my pension. Literally the definition of living the dream—for a guy like me, anyway. And after the way I'd grown up, with nothing but the clothes on my back, I thanked God every day for the opportunities the Marine Corps had given me.

"I'll tell you one thing," Brooks said, laying back down and staring at the ceiling, "you're gonna love the dating scene in Fort Worth. Much better than San Diego."

I rolled my eyes. "And what could you possibly know about that? You got married at eighteen."

"First of all, I married a Texas girl. Girls from Texas are ... different. They're loyal. Come hell or high water, my girl is always there, having my back. I may not have any experience dating in San Diego, but I've watched you get your heart stomped on for the last couple years, so it doesn't look fun."

He wasn't wrong. I'd been dating in San Diego without much success for the entire two and a half years I'd been stationed there. There were a few times I thought I'd found the real thing, but I'd been wrong each and every time. I thought we'd had the kind of love you wrote home about. Not that I had anyone at home to write to. But maybe that was the problem—I was so desperate to find "the one" that it drove them away.

I sighed. "What you have with Cat isn't normal. You guys did the whole high school sweethearts thing and got married on your boot camp leave. That should've crashed and burned."

"And yet, here we are, eight years later and better than ever." He held his arms out wide and puffed out his chest. Then he hung his head. "And trust me, it wasn't the usual high school sweethearts deal. There was a time when Cat *really* didn't like me. But that's a story for another day."

"Can't wait to hear it," I said.

Brooks and his wife had always seemed completely perfect together. They fought like, well, cats and dogs, but that seemed to be their version of flirting. I couldn't help but laugh every time I hung out with the two of them and had a front-row seat to their back-and-forth banter. I'd grown up watching a much different version of fighting between my parents.

"Don't rush it, you'll find the right girl eventually, man," Brooks offered. "And like I said, Texas girls are the best. Maybe you just need one of them instead of the girls from San Diego you keep striking out with."

"Only Texans think everything in Texas is the best," Hawkins said as he and Mills joined us.

"Yeah," Mills added. "Both of us are happily married to girls from San Diego. That's two against one."

"Pipe down, both of you," I said, not bothering to look at them. "The last time you guys tried to set me up with a girl from San Diego, she wound up being the craziest of all."

The girl had been a cousin of Hawk's wife, Ellie, and they'd set me up with her at their wedding. It took me weeks to get rid of her after that night. We'd barely talked at the wedding so I had no idea what she even saw in me to keep after me like that. It was creepy. Ellie insisted she was a cool person, but I knew she only thought that because she'd never dated the girl.

"You know what you should do?" Brooks said, sitting up again.

I looked over at him with a raised brow. "What's that?"

"You should change your settings on Connect to look for girls in Fort Worth."

I shared a confused look with Hawk and Mills, then turned my gaze back to Brooks. "But I'm not even there yet."

"What are you gonna do, keep talking to girls in San Diego?" Brooks asked. "You heard Master Guns. You're good to start checking out when we get back from deployment. What's your plan? Find a girl in San Diego, then move her to Fort Worth a few months later?"

Hawk chuckled. "Or you could do the long-distance thing. Everybody loves that."

I made a face at Hawk. "Ugh. I have bad enough luck in the same city. Long-distance dating sounds terrible."

Mills took a seat next to me on my rack. "He might have a point. Are you still using Connect?"

I shrugged. "Not since we left San Diego."

"Might as well see if you hit it off with anyone in Fort Worth. You can just tell them you're on deployment and moving there soon," Mills said.

"Bets on how long it takes for Murphy to fall in love with a Texas girl?" Hawk asked.

I rolled my eyes as Mills and Brooks threw out guesses. My friends constantly ragged on me for how fast and hard I fell for a girl, only to find out she wasn't the one. They just didn't get it. They had people. They had their wives, of course, but they had parents or siblings or freaking cousins who cared about them. I had ... well, I just had them.

Brooks patted the side of my knee. "Bro, do me a favor and let me know if you're about to fall for some girl from Fort Worth. Chances are, if she's around our age, I'll either know her, or know someone who knows her."

I blew out a breath. "I have to admit, it's not a terrible idea."

"Yeah, buddy," Brooks said, rubbing his hands together. "And again, Texas girls are—"

"The best," Mills, Hawk, and I finished for him, rolling our eyes.

He pointed at each of us and nodded. "You know it."

I pulled my phone out of my pocket and opened the dating app. "Might as well do this now. The chow hall doesn't open for dinner for another hour."

"Seriously?" Hawk checked his watch and groaned. "I'm starving."

"You're always starving," Mills said, then turned back to me as I scrolled through some of the available girls in Fort Worth. "Anyone good?"

I tilted my head from side to side, not wanting to admit how hot some of these girls were. Brooks didn't need any more fuel to his everything's-better-in-Texas fire. "A few promising ones, for sure."

"Lemme see that," Brooks said, snatching the phone out of my hand. "Oh, yes, see? This is exactly what I meant. Man, I love living vicariously through you, Murph."

I laughed, realization dawning on me as I plucked the phone out of my best friend's hand. "Ha. I guess marrying your high school sweetheart has its draw-backs, huh?"

"I guess that means I married my middle school sweetheart?" Mills asked.

I pursed my lips. "I forgot you and Brooks both have a story like that. And Hawk, you married your child-hood best friend. Look at you guys, handing out advice. What would you know about dating?"

Hawk waved a hand at me. "Man, you didn't even know me before Ellie. I went out with tons of girls before her. It's not all it's cracked up to be."

I swallowed, still smiling, but knowing he was right. It really wasn't. "You were in high school. Doesn't count."

"Man, don't get me wrong," Brooks said as Hawkins glared at me, "it's fun seeing the girls you're dating and all that. But you get rejected way more than

I ever have, and that part can't be fun. Better you than me."

Mills chuckled. "I agree with Brooks. Olivia and I have had our issues, but one thing I've never had to worry about is if the girl I love, loves me back. You fall for every girl with a pulse, and then get your heart broken, buddy. I don't envy you."

My brows snapped together. "I get it. Take it easy."

For a minute, I tried to sit there and let their ribbing go in one ear and out the other. After all, I'd started with calling them out for being so ... taken. But there was only so much I could take without wanting to punch one of them in his stupid, happily-married face. I stood from my rack and grabbed for my beanie off the blanket next to Mills. He was sitting on part of it so I yanked it out from underneath him, my cheeks turning red at their laughter over my clumsy escape from their jokes.

"Ah, Murph," Brooks called to my retreating back. "We love you, bro!"

"Yeah, yeah," I replied, letting the door to our squad bay slam shut on my way out. I didn't know where I planned to go while I waited for the chow hall to open, but anywhere was better than the humiliation I faced in there.

I shuddered against the icy wind and headed toward the chow hall. I figured I could be the first one in and start shoveling food in my face to avoid talking about this with my friends again. There was a picnic table outside the doors of the building where we ate, so I stepped up on the bench and plopped my butt on top of the table to wait.

Pulling out my phone, I opened the dating app with a sigh. I hadn't been able to Favorite any of the new girls in my feed since I'd switched my settings, and now was as good a time as any. My thumb scrolled through the pictures, tapping the heart icon on the corner of a couple girls just based on their looks alone. I didn't do that often, but some were worth a heart right off the bat. I calculated what time it was in Texas. Since it was about half past five on a Thursday evening in Japan, that made it what, three thirty Thursday morning there? These girls were either going to think I was looking for a booty call or that I had a serious sleep disorder.

A face stopped my scroll, and I sucked in a breath. She had long brown hair and a smile that I could only describe as the sweetest thing I'd ever seen. There was something about her that looked ... right. I shook my head. She wasn't even a real possibility yet, just a picture on my phone. She might not even actually look like that. It *was* online dating, after all. I forced myself not to get my hopes up and clicked on her profile to read more about her.

I pursed my lips. Her name was Ivy. She was a freaking kindergarten teacher, which explained the sweetness in her smile. Anyone who could wrangle a bunch of five-year-olds all day had to be a saint or something. Not that I had much experience with kids. I continued to browse her profile, eager to learn more about this teacher named Ivy.

Her bio said she loved to read, which didn't surprise me, considering her profession. I wasn't much of a reader. Unless you counted reading sports articles on the ESPN app. I wondered if she was into bookish guys who talked about literature and stuff over fancy coffee drinks. I preferred talking about, well, basically anything other than literature over energy drinks.

I rolled my shoulders as if to shake off the self-conscious thoughts. She was a kindergarten teacher not a college professor, maybe she didn't even like classic literature. Or coffee. Why was I acting like such a weirdo after only browsing her profile? We hadn't even Connected yet and this girl already had me all up in my own head.

Before I could talk myself out of it, I tapped the heart icon on the corner of her profile. And simply to prove to myself that I wasn't already falling for this kindergarten teacher before even talking to her, I spent the next ten minutes tapping on about two dozen other heart icons. I had no idea how many Connections would come from all of those requests, but at least it would give me something exciting to look forward to. And who knew, maybe it would be cool to have the modern version of a pen pal for this deployment.

The chow hall doors opened with a bang behind me, so I hopped off the table and headed inside, eager for some warmth. As I slipped the phone back in my pocket, I swallowed back the urge to check and see if any Connections were made yet. All those Texas girls were likely still sleeping. Especially ones who had to get up early and teach kindergarten.

3

IVY

"Did you check for any new Connections this morning?" Nora asked as we gathered our stuff to head to work.

"Not yet, I woke up late," I replied. "Have you seen the keys? I thought I put them back on the hook."

Rachel pulled them out of her pocket. "Got 'em. I'll drive, you check your app."

I rolled my eyes at her wink and followed my friends out the door. Nora cleared her throat at me, and I wrinkled my nose. "You mean now?"

She gave me a look. "We're not getting any younger."

"You're so bossy," I teased, heaving my bag onto the passenger floorboard. Judging by the weight of it, I really needed to go through that thing this weekend.

Gathering my long, floral skirt in my hands, I got in the car and pulled out my phone. I opened the Connect app and felt a jab of unease at the sight of the notifications bar. I had three new Connection Requests and three new messages.

After about a week of using it, I was better at navigating the app, but still terrible about replying without overthinking it. My girlfriends were great about helping me sound cool and collected when in reality I was anything but. Yes, this was highly deceptive. The poor guy on the other end of the message thought he was getting someone who had some chill, when in fact, I did not. But according to Nora and Rachel, talking on the phone or meeting up was a better way to tell if you had chemistry anyway.

"Okay," I said, taking a deep breath, "the first message is from Robby."

I felt a blush creep up my neck as my friends let out excited squeals. Robby and I had been messaging back and forth pretty consistently since that first night. Nothing too serious, just get-to-know-you type questions. But he was definitely the front-runner, if there was one.

"What does it say?" Rachel asked from the driver's seat, merging onto the highway.

I opened the message and read it out loud, not bothering to screen it first to see if I should. This whole

Connect situation had become a team sport, and my friends had been privy to pretty much every message so far.

Robby: Would you want to meet up for coffee this weekend? It's my ex's weekend with my son.

Nora made a face. "I have to ask ... are you okay with the kid thing?"

"The 'kid thing,' Nora? *Really*?" Rachel said, shooting her a look in the rearview mirror.

"I'm just asking," Nora said, holding up her hands. "It could come with some baby mama drama."

I understood why this was a triggering topic for Rachel. She'd been raised by a single dad after her mom had left them when she was five. Being a kindergarten teacher and spending every day around kids that age, I couldn't imagine any parent being able to do that. It was such a fun age. So inquisitive and amusing. I cried every year on the last day of school, knowing my students were about to move on to first grade. I couldn't fathom the idea of leaving one of my own children forever.

I swallowed. "I mean, I love kids. And like I told him that night, it's not a deal breaker by itself. But I did wonder about his ex."

"Let's hold off and see what else you have in there," Rachel suggested.

She was right. I had no idea if I was ready to meet

up with Robby, and we were almost to our school. If we were going to have time to check out the rest of my notifications, we'd have to move on. I backed out of the message with him and scanned the other two unread ones. They were quick replies from two of the other guys I was talking to, and since I didn't need my friends to help me answer them, I quickly responded to each and then returned to the main menu.

"Next up," I said with a wag of my eyebrows, "three new Connection Requests."

Nora rubbed her hands together. "My favorite part."

I laughed, opening the folder of requests. "The first one's cute. His name is Aaron, and it says here he's a minor league baseball player."

"Yes," Rachel said, hitting the steering wheel for emphasis. "Accept!"

Nora flicked her shoulder from her spot in the back seat. "This is *not* your show, Workout Barbie."

I chuckled. "He is cute, though."

Nora peered over my shoulder. "Okay, yeah, accept."

I tapped the heart on Aaron's profile and a big box popped up to let me know we'd made a Connection. I moved on to the next request and wrinkled my nose. He was far from my type based on looks, but I tried my best to ignore that until I checked his profile. I really, really didn't want to be too objectifying with this whole thing. There was more to love than just looks.

"This one is Matthew," I told my friends, scrolling through his profile. "He looks … nice. He's a manager at Target."

"Ooh, hello discounts," Nora said. "Lemme see."

She leaned forward and looked at the profile as I tilted my screen back toward her so she could see it. I stifled a laugh when she made a similar face to what I must have made. Again, I felt bad for being superficial, but judging by Nora's reaction, I wasn't the only one who didn't find him attractive.

"Hmm," Nora said, sitting back in here seat.

"Lemme see," Rachel said as she came to a stop at a light. She slipped her sporty sunglasses down the bridge of her nose and peered at my phone. "Well, IDK, Vee. Maybe he's nice. But you don't have to decide right now. Come back to him later."

Grateful that I didn't have to nix poor Manager Matthew based entirely on his looks, I moved to the last Connection Request and my stomach flipped when I saw his face. Now, *this* guy was handsome. It was the first word that popped into my head. Not cute, not hot. Handsome. In a way that had me swooning over him before I even knew his name. Was it his eyes? They were so blue I could clearly see the color even though it wasn't a close-up of his face. Or maybe it was his smile. He had the kind of smile that told me I could trust him with my heart, but that he also liked to have fun and be flirty. I wasn't sure exactly how a smile could say all of that, but his did. And it was melting me.

"Uh, hello? Earth to Ivy?" Nora tapped me on the shoulder with probably more force than necessary. "Lemme see!"

I blinked rapidly to snap myself out of my trance and turned the phone around, surprised to see that we'd already parked in one of the designated spots reserved for teachers. I hadn't even noticed we'd pulled into the lot. How long had I been staring into that guy's dreamy eyes? And how could a picture make me feel butterflies before I even knew anything about him? Or if he was even real ….

"He's cute," Nora said, grabbing my wrist and angling the phone toward Rachel so she could see.

"Agreed," Rachel said.

I yanked my hand back and let out a huff. He wasn't just cute. He was … more. I didn't know what he was, but he was messing with my head already. I needed to learn more. I scrolled down, eagerness making my thumb shake as it hovered over the screen.

"It says his name is Jake Murphy," I read to my friends. "Crap. He's a Marine."

Nora and Rachel both laughed, and Rachel said, "Oh, boy."

"You don't think he knows Travis, do you?" I asked, my eyes wide.

Rachel waved her hand. "That would be a big coincidence."

"Or an act of God," Nora said, "dooming you to fall for another one of your brother's friends."

I rolled my eyes. "Literally my nightmare."

Rachel looked toward the school and checked her watch. "We have to go soon. What else does it say?"

"Crap. You guys. It says he's stationed in San Diego but moving here this summer. Travis is stationed in San Diego." I blinked at my friends. "He seriously might know him."

"San Diego is a military town," Nora said, her tone reassuring. "There's probably thousands of Marines there. Don't get ahead of yourself. Besides, Travis is on deployment. If this guy's profile said he was on deployment, then I'd be worried."

I let out a shaky breath. The last thing I needed was to start dating another one of my brother's friends. Last time was supposed to be the only time. And he was only okay with it after what felt like years of time passing. When Cory dumped me and moved to New York, he hadn't even told Travis about it. Travis heard from Mom, who told him how heartbroken I was. Their friendship was destroyed. And even though he wouldn't admit it, I knew Travis blamed me for losing his best friend.

"Okay," Rachel said, opening her car door. "Time to go, friends."

Nora and I followed her out of the car, but my nose was still buried in Jake's profile. His hobbies seemed pretty typical. According to his bio, he liked video games and wanted to weed out anyone who would hate that. I laughed to myself, knowing that was a thing with some girls. Me, I didn't mind it. Cory used to play video games for hours while I'd read a book or do my lesson plans at the coffee table. I liked to think of it as togetherness and independence wrapped in one. I could definitely see myself falling into the same relaxed relationship style with this handsome Marine, too.

Jake's profile also said that he was a Christian under religious preferences, a fact that I liked since I'd noticed some guys chose to leave that section blank. His favorite food was pizza, as was mine. He liked football and tailgating, which was something I used to do with Cory and all of his friends. Did this mean I had a type? And that Jake was it? Because I wouldn't mind continuing to have tailgating parties and watch Sunday football with a new boyfriend.

Ah, screw it. From what I could tell by his bio alone, Jake had serious potential. Sure, the fact that he was a Marine was risky as heck. He very well could know my brother, and that could come back to bite me. But it was worth a shot. And if he did wind up knowing Travis, I'd tell him I couldn't get involved with one of my brother's friends, and we'd end it before it went anywhere. No biggie. I took a deep breath and tapped the heart next to Jake's gorgeous smile. As I slipped my phone into my bag and followed my friends into the school, I said a silent prayer that Jake Murphy had never met another Marine named Travis Brooks.

It was all I could do to keep my phone tucked away in my bag until lunch. I wanted to see if Jake had messaged me now that we'd made the Connection, but I knew it was wrong. Messing around on a dating app while I was supposed to be shaping young minds was a big no-no as far as I was concerned. But as soon as my littles were safely handed off to the lunch aid, I made a beeline for my desk and whipped out my bag.

My heart pounded as I opened the app and saw that I had two new messages. Praying one was from Jake, I tapped the icon and bit my lip. Sure enough, one from Robby, and one from the handsome Marine with the bright-blue eyes.

I opened Jake's message and smiled as I read it.

Jake: Hey, Ivy. My name's Jake, but not from State Farm. How are you?

It was short, yes. But it was funny. Or at least, I

thought it was funny. It was cheesy in the best way. He'd sent the message several hours earlier, but I typed out a quick reply, hoping he was still online so we could chat.

Me: Does that mean you're not wearing khakis? I'm great, how are you?

Sitting in my chair, I fidgeted with the PopSocket on the back of my phone case. I hoped he didn't think my reply was too forward. It had just come to me, and I'd sent it without overthinking it for once. As the minutes ticked by, I worried I'd messed up. Would he think I was dumb? No, he wouldn't, he was the one who made the State Farm joke in the first place. I wondered if he made that joke with every girl or if I was special. I scoffed out loud. Why would I be special? He didn't even know me. Then again, I didn't even know him, and here I was, acting like a total loon.

To take my mind off of Jake—and prove to myself that I wasn't obsessing over him so quickly—I went back to Robby's message. He apologized for coming on too strong about meeting up. He must have figured my lack of response earlier meant I didn't want to. Did I want to? The whole idea of meeting up with a guy from this app freaked me out. On the one hand, he could be a serial killer. On the other, he could be a total jerk. And worst of all, maybe I'd be super into him and he'd be super repelled by me. I leaned back in my chair and rested my neck on the back, staring straight up at the ceiling. Online dating was exhausting.

My phone buzzed in my hand and I jumped, fumbling to catch it before it slipped from my grasp. It was a Connect message. And since I hadn't replied to Robby yet, I knew it must be Jake. I cleared my throat, tucked my hair behind my ear, and sat up a little straighter.

Jake: Are you asking me what I'm wearing?

I felt heat rise up my cheeks. I needed to steer this conversation to a safe zone—and fast—before he got the wrong idea about me. I typed out a response, deleted it, tried again, and deleted it once more. Then, with a tight smile, I decided to be myself.

Me: Let's start over. Hi, I'm Ivy. I'm completely new to online dating and totally embarrassed by the direction of this conversation. Nice to meet you.

I hit Send and waited, then let out a breath I hadn't realized I'd been holding when I saw the chat bubble appear to let me know he was already typing back.

Jake: Hi, Ivy. It's nice to meet you, too. Are you from Fort Worth originally?

Me: Yes, born and raised. Where are you from?

Jake: Portland, Oregon. Are you a cat person or a dog person? (This is important)

Me: Dog person ... you?

Jake: Same.

I smiled at the dog emoji he'd included at the end of his message. Before I could think of a reply, he sent another message.

Jake: Do you have any dogs or do you just like them better in theory?

Me: In theory. You?

Jake: Same. Can't have a dog in the barracks. Someday, though.

My thumb hovered over the keyboard. I had no idea what to say next. I could ask him how his day was going. But what if it was going poorly? Maybe he wouldn't want to talk about it. Ooh, food. According to my roomies, food was a great topic for guys.

Me: Your bio said you live in San Diego. Are you having Mexican food for lunch? The Mexican food there is amazing.

There was a pause, and I wondered if I'd said something wrong. Finally, the chat bubbles appeared as he typed out his reply.

Jake: I'm on kind of a weird schedule right now, so it's not lunchtime for me. It's sleep time. But yes, the Mexican food in San Diego is legit.

He didn't need to elaborate. Having a brother in the Marines meant I was used to hearing about their constant readiness. Sometimes Travis would get assigned to the night crew and he'd keep opposite hours from the rest of us. I figured Jake must be on night crew. I wanted to say something about it to impress him with my military knowledge, but I thought better of it.

Me: Sorry if I woke you up! You'll have to grab some Tex-Mex to compare them when you move here.

Jake: It's okay, I'm a really light sleeper. What's the difference?

Me: I'm not much of a cook so I can't tell you specifics, but Tex-Mex is better.

Jake: You have me rolling. You really are from Texas. You said you're new to online dating. What made you sign up?

I slumped back in my chair. Another thing I wanted to lie about but knew I shouldn't.

Me: Honestly?

Jake: Of course.

Me: My friends pushed me into it.

Jake: If it makes you feel any better, that's pretty common.

Me: Is that why you signed up?

Jake: No. I signed up because all of my buddies are in relationships and I was having really bad luck trying to meet girls in real life.

Me: That's honest.

Jake: That's how I roll.

Me: You've been on here for a while then? How's it working out for you?

Jake: Right now, I think it's going well.

My heart fluttered. This guy was good.

Jake: So ... you're a teacher, right? What do you like to do on the weekends? Do you have to grade a lot of papers?

Me: I teach kindergarten, so it's more like cutting out gingerbread men. And I live with my two best friends, who are also teachers, so we usually hang out and do our prep work together.

Jake: All work and no play? What do you do for fun?

I paused. When I was with Cory, my weekends were full of football parties and barbecues with Cory and all of his friends. *Our* friends. But ever since we'd broken up, I'd lost all of those friends because they were connected to him through his firehouse. Thank God for Rachel and Nora. I couldn't tell Jake any of that, however. I'd admitted that my friends had pushed me into this, but he hadn't asked why. Better to save the breakup talk for later, right? Should I make something up to sound more fun? I shook my head. If this was going to work, I needed to be myself. I didn't have to talk to him about the breakup yet, but I didn't have to lie outright.

Me: Working is fun when you love what you do :)
Jake: Touché.

Me: How about you? Are you moving here because you're getting out of the Marines?

Jake: I am, but I'll be doing pretty much the same job at the JRB out there by you. Only difference will be that I'll be a civilian contractor instead of a Marine.

Me: You must like your job. What do you do?

Jake: I work on F-18s.

Alarm bells went off in my head. No way. I didn't know much about Travis's job in the Marines, but I knew without a doubt that he worked on F-18s because I'd posed for a picture in front of one when I'd visited him in San Diego last summer.

"What are you doing?" a voice called from my classroom door, making me jump.

I put a hand over my heart, relaxing when I saw Nora's head poking through the opening. "Girl. You scared the crap out of me."

She entered the room with Rachel on her heels. "We brought your lunch."

"We were in the lounge waiting for you," Rachel said, plopping my lunch bag on my desk along with her own.

My friends made themselves at home around my desk, and we unpacked our bags. Meal prepping was a routine on Sunday afternoons. I internally scolded myself, realizing I could have told Jake about it when he'd asked about my weekend stuff. Though, I guess "meal prepping" wasn't that cool of an answer for what I do for fun.

Every Sunday afternoon, we cooked healthy meals for the week and packed them in color-coded containers to bring to work. It saved us a ton of money and the meals were usually good, but if it weren't for Nora and Rachel, I would never be able to stay consistent with it. It was a fun thing to do with friends, but I wasn't that into cooking. That was Nora's deal. And I definitely wasn't the color-coded organization type. That bit of OCD was provided by Rachel. My contribution to the whole thing was doing the coupon clipping and grocery shopping, since if it were up to those two, we'd go way over budget.

"What were you doing in here?" Nora asked, sticking a bite of grilled chicken in her mouth.

"I was talking to that Marine from earlier," I replied. "And I feel bad because he must be on night crew. He said he'd been sleeping."

Nora stabbed her fork in Rachel's direction. "Told you she was talking to him."

"You did," Rachel said with a chuckle, then turned to me. "How's it going?"

"It's going well. I think. He seems easy to talk to."

"Why do I feel like there's a 'but' coming?" Nora asked.

I poked around at the food in my container. "He just told me he works with F-18s. And so does Travis."

Rachel and Nora made similarly sketched out faces at me.

I stuck out my bottom lip. "I'll have to find out if they know each other and go from there. And if they do, I'll tell him we can't keep talking."

"Or," Nora said, "you could keep talking to him and not even ask. I mean, if the conversation is going well and you kinda like him, why ruin it?"

Rachel rolled her eyes. "Uh, several reasons. If Travis knows him and doesn't like him, drama. If Travis knows him and does like him, drama. Better to find out now than later."

I gestured to Rachel with my water bottle. "I'm with her. I finally feel like Travis and I are getting back to normal, and it's been almost a year since Cory left. I don't want to mess anything up again. In fact, I'll casually bring it up right now."

Me: That's cool. My brother is actually a Marine. He works on F-18s, too.

I put the phone down and turned back to my lunch. "There. I brought it up."

"Fingers crossed," Rachel said, giving me a half smile.

"I would've let it go longer," Nora said, with a sly smile. "But what do I know?"

4

JAKE

A brother who's a Marine and works on F-18s? The Marine Corps was getting smaller the longer I was in it. And the Air Wing of the Marine Corps was even worse. These days, there were only three Marine bases you could be stationed at if you worked on the F-18 Hornet. Marine Corps Air Station Miramar in San Diego, MCAS Beaufort in South Carolina, and MCAS Iwakuni in Japan. The chances of me knowing her brother were pretty dang high, considering I'd been stationed at both Beaufort and San Diego before, and I was currently at the base in Japan on deployment. Unless, of course, he worked at the JRB in Fort Worth and he was a reservist or something. In which case, I might not know him yet, but I'd likely start working with him this summer.

I yawned. Thanks to the time difference between Forth Worth and Japan, I'd been woken up around two in the morning by her message. I'd always been a light sleeper, but since I'd fallen asleep with my phone on my chest, the vibration had jolted me awake. Though it was brief, I felt like we'd had a good conversation. I hadn't needed to think too hard about any of my answers. That is, until she'd asked about whether it was lunchtime in San Diego.

It was probably dumb, but I really didn't want to tell her I was on deployment yet. That revelation would likely lead to her asking where I was deployed. And although it was highly unlikely she was a member of ISIS masquerading as a kindergarten teacher, I wanted to get to know her at least a little bit more before I revealed any troop movement.

There had been a long break in the conversation right after I'd told her I worked on F-18s, so I'd fallen asleep. When I woke up and saw her message about her brother, I understood why there'd been the pause. If her brother worked on F-18s, she was probably wondering the same thing I was. Did we know each other? I checked my phone again to see if she'd written back yet after I asked where he was stationed. Nope. But it had only been about an hour, so hopefully she would soon.

I stood on the catwalk that overlooked the huge

hangar. It housed several of our jets and various work-stations. Marines were everywhere, working in groups on various projects. I recognized the guys from my unit as they worked alongside guys who were stationed there in Japan. I'd met a few of them, but most of them I didn't recognize. Any of them could be her brother.

I checked my phone again, disappointed to see that I still didn't have any new notifications.

"You on that app again?" Hawk asked, coming up behind me and popping open a Japanese soda.

I evaded his question and nodded at the beverage. "Where'd you get that?"

"The gedunk," he replied, hooking his thumb over his shoulder and referring to the snack room of the hangar. It was aptly named back in the thirties for the sound the vending machines made when they dispensed the food. "They were restocked last night."

"Sweet, I'll have to grab one," I said. "So ... one of the girls I'm talking to on Connect has a brother who works on F-18s."

Hawk tilted his head and looked up. "For real?"

"What's up, guys?" Mills greeted us as he came up the stairs from the main floor. He pointed at Hawk's soda. "Hey, where'd you get that?"

"The gedunk," we both replied.

"Man, they were sold out last time I checked." Mills lamented. "What were you guys talking about?"

I scratch the back of my neck. "There's this girl ..."

"Ha." Mills chuckled. "Always."

"Shut up," I said, pulling my phone out of my pocket. "She says her brother's a Marine and works with F-18s. I wonder if we know the guy."

Mills nodded at the phone. "I'm sure we could do a little recon and figure it out. Let's see her."

I opened the app and went to Ivy's profile, both Hawk and Mills hovered over my shoulder. Mills frowned, then pulled out his own phone. "Ivy? Wait a minute. Bro. And she lives in Fort Worth? If that's who I think it is, you've got a huge problem."

"You know who her brother is?" I asked, watching him scroll through his phone.

"Oh, man," Mills said, his eyes wide as he looked at his phone. "Yup. And, so do you."

With a look that could only be described as pity, Mills turned his phone around to face me and Hawk. It was a family photo posted on social media. My eyes immediately landed on Ivy, her pretty brown hair pulled to one side and falling over her shoulder. She had one hand on her hip and the other wrapped around an older woman who must be her mom. Next to the mom was an older man, her father most likely. And next to him, with a wide smile, was Brooks.

"What the ... Brooks? Come on," I said, shaking my

head and whisper-shouting just in case my buddy was near.

"Trust me, that's her," Mills said. "I met her last year when Brooks and I were in the hospital at Walter Reed and then again when his family came to visit. You guys were still on that deployment."

I swallowed, remembering what he called his sister. "Vee. Vee is short for Ivy. I didn't even think twice about it."

"*Ding-ding-ding*," Mills said.

Hawk whistled and patted me on the shoulder. "Don't beat yourself up, man. What are the chances?"

"I can't believe it. Of all people. It was his idea to switch my settings to Fort Worth," I defended myself, glancing over the railing to see if I could see Brooks working down below.

"Yeah, but I bet he didn't know his sister was on the app or he probably would have told you to steer clear. What are you going to do?" Hawk asked.

"What kind of question is that?" Mills shot a glance over his shoulder and lowered his voice. "What can he do? Brooks would kill him if he found out he was talking to his sister. Murphy, seriously. I saw it with my own eyes. He's ridiculously protective of her. He'd kill you."

Hawk snorted. "Oh, come on. Brooks knows

Murphy's a good guy. It could be way worse. He's not a player or anything."

"Oh, sure," Mills nodded, sarcasm dripping from his tone. "This guy falls in love with every girl he meets. You think Brooks wants him to fall for his baby sister? Get outta here with that."

"Has he talked to you guys about Cory?" I asked them, picking at the edges of my phone case. My friends shared a look and shook their heads at me, so I took a deep breath and slipped the phone back in my pocket. "He was Brooks's best friend back in Fort Worth. A firefighter. Friends their whole lives."

"Okay ..." Hawk said, crossing his arms.

"Cory was with Vee for years. The three of them were close. And then one day he dumps her and moves to New York."

Mills whistled.

"I guess he got some job offer in the city," I continued. "He told Vee he didn't want to stay in his hometown forever and marry the only girl he'd ever been with."

"Ouch." Hawk cringed, then chuckled when Mills rolled his eyes.

"Yep. And Cory didn't even tell Brooks about it. Brooks found out from their mom," I finished.

Hawk shook his head. "Guessing they're not cool anymore?"

"Nope," I said.

"How do you know all of this anyway?" Mills asked, putting a hand on the railing and looking over the edge, undoubtedly checking for Brooks.

"Because Brooks was all messed up about it." I shuffled my feet.

"Man, and now another one of his friends is into his sister," Hawk said, almost shrinking away from the idea.

"I'm not into his sister," I said. "I've had one conversation with her."

"Good. Then it shouldn't be a big deal for you to not talk to her again now that you know," Mills said.

I shrugged. "Yeah, I mean, it's not a big deal at all."

Hawk leaned back against the railing. "Eh, you know what? I say go for it."

Mills and I looked at Hawk like he had two heads.

"I'm serious," Hawk continued. "So, it didn't work out for his friend and his sister last time. Doesn't mean it won't work out this time. I stayed away from Ellie thanks to some pointless family drama and it didn't wind up mattering in the end."

"Hawk," Mills said, "this is not the same thing as the boneheaded moves you made with Ellie. I was there."

"Fine," Hawk said, holding out his hands in defeat. "I guess I just feel bad for our friend, here."

Mills wrinkled his nose. "Don't feel bad for him.

He's fine. There are plenty of girls in Fort Worth for you to talk to, am I right?

I nodded. "Yeah, of course."

My phone vibrated in my pocket signaling I had a message. I didn't pull it out or react to it. Considering everything I'd just learned, I knew if it was Ivy, I shouldn't even open it. Mills was right. There were plenty of girls in Fort Worth, and Brooks would kill me if his sister was the one I chose to talk to. After everything that happened the last time his friend dated his sister, it would be a low blow to go there. And these guys were the closest thing I had to family. I didn't want to do anything to mess that up.

And yet, there was some unexplainable pull that made my fingers itch to grab for my phone. Man, was I in trouble.

"Hey, Murph," Brooks called to me from the lunch line at the chow hall.

I'd just walked in the door and was more than ready for a lunch break. We'd been gearing up for a training exercise and needed seventeen jets to be loaded with ordnance. The F-18 carried nine different types of weapons. As ordnancemen, or ordies, we were in charge of making sure they were safely built, loaded, and ready to drop. I'd already put out at least a dozen metaphorical fires related to our mission for the day, and I was exhausted.

"Hey, man," I said as I joined my friend in line, guilt settling in my gut knowing I still had a message from his sister sitting unread in my inbox. "Did Hawk and Mills already come through?"

Brooks shook his head. "Nah, I had them finish loading twenty-one before they could break for chow."

"Good," I replied.

Jet number twenty-one had given us the most trouble that morning, so I was glad he'd made sure it was getting finished. Since Brooks and I were sergeants and our other two buddies were corporals, they did more of the wrench turning, while we did more of the delegating.

I pulled out my to-do list for the afternoon and shook my head. "It's gonna be a long day."

"Ugh," Brooks said, looking at the words written on the small notebook in my hand. "Put that away. I don't want to think about it for at least an hour."

I snorted. "Try thirty minutes."

He hung his head. "I'll be glad when we finish up here and move on to the next base. I heard we'll have some shorter days in Korea."

"Better weather, too?"

"Nope," Brooks replied. "We'll still be out there in

the cold. Well, not as much as Hawk and Mills. But still."

"At least we have Hawaii to look forward to," I said, patting him on the back as we moved up in line and grabbed trays for the buffet. "A week in paradise will be just what we need after this."

"One hundred percent."

We moved through the line and took food from the maroon containers organized by type of dish. There were meats, sides, salads, and desserts. Not gourmet cuisine by most people's standards, but it was a step above a lot of the cafeteria food I'd eaten during my time in the Marine Corps. They even had a sushi section at the end with fresh sushi, rice, and miso soup. Compared to what I grew up eating—or not eating—it was one of those hundred-dollar buffets at Caesar's Palace.

As I scooped food onto my plate next to Brooks, my mind traveled to Ivy. I still couldn't believe that out of all of the good-looking Texas girls I'd seen while scrolling that app, hers was the profile that caught my attention the most.

I snuck a look at my friend. I didn't see much of a family resemblance. Then again, I didn't look much like my older brother, either. I knew I needed to tread lightly, but I was still curious to know more about her.

"So," I said, clearing my throat as I filled my tray, "how's the family?"

Brooks shrugged. "Fine, I guess. My mom said she and my sister sent a care package, so that should be here soon. It takes what, three weeks?"

"Yeah, I think so. That's nice of them."

"My mom said my sister's students made me cards," he continued, making my stomach turn as I noticed he'd now mentioned her twice but never said her name. No wonder I hadn't realized who she was. "She's a kindergarten teacher."

I swallowed. "Oh, is she? Cool. I don't think you ever told me that."

Brooks paid for his tray of food and looked around the room for a table. He chose one and gestured to it with his tray. "I'll be over there."

I nodded with a stiff smile, then turned to the cashier to pay for my lunch. I was in dangerous waters and I'd only had one conversation with the girl. It was clear I needed to put an end to this before it got any further and I actually had something to feel guilty about. Still, Ivy was a real person. And she was obviously a caring person, since she had her kindergarten students make cards for her deployed brother. Even though we couldn't possibly keep talking, she deserved more than being blown off with no explanation.

As I walked toward the table Brooks had selected, I

balanced my tray in one hand and pulled out my phone. I navigated to the app and opened Ivy's unread reply to my question about where her brother was stationed. A question I'd been able to answer on my own, unfortunately.

Ivy: He's stationed in San Diego but he's on deployment right now. I'd tell you where but I don't think we're supposed to talk about that kind of stuff, right?

I smiled to myself at her knowledge of operational security. At some point, Brooks must have briefed her on how much she was allowed to tell people about his whereabouts. It was the reason I'd put that I was stationed in San Diego on my profile but had left off the part about being on deployment. It wasn't a secret necessarily, but it wasn't something I needed to advertise on my profile for everyone to see.

I was almost to Brooks's table, so I typed out a quick reply to Ivy and slipped my phone back in my pocket with a sigh. It was a shame. She really was gorgeous.

5

IVY

Jake: It's okay, you don't have to tell me where he's deployed ... I'm here with him. Long story short, I know your brother.

"What the ..." I said from my spot on the couch, making my roomies look over with curious expressions. "Guys. Jake knows Trav."

Nora and Rachel looked at each other with wide eyes, then Nora came over and sat next to me, pulling my throw blanket up and around her own legs to settle in for my drama. I handed her the phone so she could read the conversation and buried my face in my hands as she read it out loud to Rachel.

"Seriously?" Rachel exclaimed when Nora had finished reading. "What are the freaking odds?"

"I know," I mumbled.

"What are you going to say?" Nora asked, handing me back my phone.

I stretched my neck. "I guess I could ask him how they know each other ... maybe they only met once or something."

Nora nodded. "Yeah, do that. Maybe it won't even be an issue."

Me: You do? Small world. How do you know him?

I sent the message and blew out a breath. "I kind of want to text Travis and ask him if he knows Jake. Maybe he won't even remember who he is."

Rachel made a face. "I wouldn't. Don't call attention to you dating again, just in case he's still all weird about the Cory thing."

"I wouldn't want to bring attention to you dating regardless of Cory," Nora added. "I've seen how protective he is about you."

My phone buzzed in my hand, and I quickly opened the message.

Jake: He's my best friend. I'm at lunch with him right now. Should I tell him you say hi?

My eyes bulged out of my head as I read the message out loud, then another message quickly appeared.

Jake: I'm kidding, BTW. Not about being at lunch with him, but about saying hi. I know better.

I couldn't help the smile that spread across my face

as I finished reading Jake's message to my friends. "He's funny. Why does he have to be funny?"

"Shut it down," Rachel warned with a short laugh. "This is not a good idea."

I groaned and pushed the blanket off my lap, getting up to pace the room. "I never should have let you guys talk me into this. I don't even know if I want to start dating, let alone deal with this mess. I don't even know how to date someone other than Cory, and I'm clearly not off to a good start if the one guy I want to talk to is off-limits."

"Vee, it's been like a year since Cory left. You're ready. We would know better than anyone," Nora said.

"I agree. We know you better than you know your-self," Rachel added. "And just because this Marine is off limits, doesn't mean you shouldn't try. Don't forget about Robby! I thought he was really promising."

Even though I'd only had one conversation with Jake, I was still bummed about not being able to explore it further. Robby had seemed promising, it was true, but I didn't get butterflies just thinking about Robby. I tapped my phone against my open palm and bit my lip.

I wondered why I'd never met Jake when visiting Travis in San Diego. It wasn't that Jake was the hottest guy I'd ever seen or anything, but there was some-thing in his eyes that captivated me. I knew I'd never seen them in real life. I definitely would have remembered.

"I guess I'll reply and let him know it can't go any further," I told my friends, heading to my bedroom. "It's almost ten, so I'm gonna do that and then head to bed."

My roommates each gave me pitying smiles, said their good nights, then turned back to the movie we'd been watching when I first got Jake's message. No wonder there were long gaps between messages from him. He was fourteen hours ahead of me. Which was also why he was eating lunch with Travis while I was about to go to sleep. For him, it was already tomorrow. That would take some getting used to. Oh, wait. No ... it wouldn't. Because we weren't going to keep talking.

I closed the door to my room and flopped down on my unmade bed. Stuffing a pillow under my chest and propping up on my elbows, I thought about how to handle this. I knew I should tell him to enjoy his lunch and that we shouldn't talk again. But there was no harm in finding out how he'd figured out who my brother was. I couldn't help but be curious about how that went down, especially if it involved Travis discovering that I was on an online dating app.

Me: This is such a small world. How did you figure it out?

I pictured my brother eating lunch across from Jake and wondered if it was hard for him to be on his phone messaging me without letting Travis know who he was talking to. Knowing my brother, he was probably on his own phone. Maybe talking to Cat or playing some dumb game or scrolling through memes. He was a guy, after all. My lunches with my girlfriends were full of chatter. But for all I knew, these two were eating together silently, both on their phones.

Jake: Long story short, our other friend, Mills, recognized you.

Me: Is that the friend I met when they were in the hospital? Matt, right?

Jake: Yeah, Matt.

Me: How's he doing? He and his wife were both really nice.

Jake: He's good. They've overcome a lot of stuff since that deployment. It was pretty rough on them.

A familiar ache took root inside of me as I thought about those days. I'd been in class when my principal had come in and told me my mom was in the office. Sure, she'd come to my school to meet me for lunch or for other perfectly ordinary reasons. But I'd never been interrupted in the middle of the day by my principal telling me she was there.

At the time, my mind had instantly flashed to my dad. I thought she was there to tell me he'd had a heart attack or something. He was healthy as a horse and swam laps in our pool every single morning, so it wasn't a realistic assumption.

My principal offered to take over in my class—while they figured out a longer-term solution—and I instantly knew I wasn't wrong to be worried. Whatever she was there to tell me would be devastating.

I'd sprinted through the halls, even catching a shrill warning from the hall monitor to use my walking feet. When I burst into the office, my mom's eyes were puffy and red from crying. My heart squeezed at the sight of her. This was a woman in pain. I knew it had to be one of her boys. It was either my dad or it was Travis. My heart sank at the realization that of the two of them, he was the more likely one to be in trouble. He was deployed in Afghanistan, after all.

The resulting conversation with my mom would be one I'd never forget as long as I lived. She'd told me Travis had been shot during an attack on the base. She hadn't known details at the time, just that she and my dad needed to fly to Germany with Travis's wife. He was on his way there for surgery and it was very touch and go. She'd apologized for not being able to bring me, but the military was only allowing his wife and parents to fly out. She promised to update me when she knew more, but for now, she wanted to take me home.

A few days later, when he'd come out of the first surgery in Germany and then went to Walter Reed

Hospital in Washington D.C., my parents had flown me there so I could be with them. His friend Matt and his wife had been getting ready to leave just as I'd arrived, so we didn't spend much time with them, just long enough to realize that Travis's friends really were like his brothers. They honestly seemed to think of him—and us, by extension—as family.

Me: I can relate. That was a scary time. Were you there?

Jake: No, I was on the aircraft carrier with the rest of our unit. They only sent your brother and Mills (Matt) to the base.

I felt like I'd known that at some point. So, Jake had known Travis for a while then, if he'd been in his unit during that deployment. Travis always referred to his group of friends as "the guys." She knew Matt because of the attack, and she thought she remembered hearing about another friend whose last name was a type of bird, maybe? But she didn't think she'd ever heard Travis mention Jake before. Unless he had a nickname. I hit my palm on my forehead. If he'd talked about Jake, he'd probably only used his last name. Which neither of us could see on the dating app.

Me: What's your last name? If Travis has ever said anything about you, he probably called you that.

Jake: It's Murphy.

Me: It does sound familiar, now that I think about

it. But I probably still wouldn't have made the connection.

Jake: **Your brother always calls you Vee. I always thought your name was Victoria or something, LOL. If I'd seen an 'Ivy Brooks' from Fort Worth upfront, I never would have messaged you.**

I bit my lip. I should not flirt with my brother's best friend. I should not. I should not.

Me: **Are you sorry you messaged me?**

The bubbles that signaled he was typing came up, disappeared, then came back again.

Jake: **I should be. But, no.**

The corners of my mouth twitched and I felt heat warm my cheeks. I'd been resistant to dating, but this feeling was addicting. I couldn't remember the last time I'd had honest-to-goodness butterflies. It wasn't that I hadn't been attracted to Cory, but we'd been together since we were kids. There was familiarity and comfort and a sense of home. But this feeling of newness was, well, new. And exciting. And I didn't want it to stop.

Me: **Maybe we can still talk. As friends.**

Jake: **Hmm ... you sure that's a good idea?**

Me: **No.**

I had to add a laughing emoji to the end of my message because I knew I was being ridiculous. I looked around my dimly lit room. It must be because it's nighttime. Everything feels more romantic and exciting at nighttime. I'd probably wake up in the morning and regret this whole conversation.

With a huff, I dropped my phone on the bed and pressed my face into my pillow. Judging by the seconds ticking by with no response from Jake, mistakes were definitely made. Finally, my phone buzzed, and I popped my head up, scrambling to open the message.

Jake: Well, I am moving there soon. Brooks said his friends would be able to show me around and stuff. Maybe you could help, too.

Me: I could. As a friend.

Jake: Cool. Thanks.

I rolled over onto my back and pressed my phone to my chest. At least we had a reason to talk. It totally wasn't that there was some unexplained pull to him that made me want to talk to my brother's best friend behind his back. No, not at all. It was that I wanted to help my brother's best friend get settled into our hometown. Like any good sister would. Like a Good Samaritan.

Me: Are you excited to move here? I bet it'll be a lot different than Portland.

Jake: I'm surprised you didn't say it's better than Portland.

Me: Oh, it is. For sure. ;)

Jake: There's that Texas girl again.

Me: I'm not as bad as Travis.

Jake: He's the worst.

Me: Agreed.

Jake: But yes, I'm excited to move there. I hear Fort Worth is good because it feels like a small town but there's a lot to do. I'm not into big cities.

Hearing Jake wasn't into big cities made my mind flash to Cory. He hadn't been much of city boy either, having been born and raised here in Fort Worth. I wondered for the hundredth—maybe thousandth—time what it was about New York City that made him want to leave. He'd left me, his family, his home ... all for a fancy firefighting gig in the city and the promise of a more exciting life. Would Jake get here and think Fort Worth was boring compared to his life in the Marines? Maybe he'd eventually want to leave, too.

I pushed the negativity out of my mind. Maybe he didn't have that wanderlust and was the type who wanted to settle down somewhere.

Me: Travis has done a lot of traveling in the Marines. Do you like to travel?

Jake: It's a pretty cool perk. Free rides all over the world. It comes with a lot of less fun stuff, too, but I try to remember it could always be worse.

I wondered what he meant by that. It was probably too soon to ask about what his idea of worse was, but I filed it away for later. I wanted to learn more about him. As a friend, of course.

Me: Have you gotten to go to a lot of interesting places?

Jake: Yeah, I guess. Maybe not a lot compared to some people. Italy, Kuwait, Afghanistan, Iraq, Bahrain. On this deployment so far, we've just done Japan but we've got some cool places coming up.

Me: That you can't tell me about, or you'd have to kill me?

Jake: Something like that ;) At least not in a message ... maybe on a video chat, though.

My heart picked up speed. Was a video chat the next step in online dating? Not like we were online dating necessarily, since we'd agreed to be friends. But if we were, and we were doing this long-distance, I imagined a video chat would be the equivalent of going out for coffee. Like on a date. When Robby had asked me to coffee, all I'd felt was apprehension. But if Jake were here in Texas and he'd asked me, I could see myself saying yes. Him being friends with Travis was a roadblock, for sure. But it was probably also what made me feel so comfortable talking to Jake. If Travis trusted him, maybe I could, too.

Me: I'd like that.

Jake: Cool. Well, we have to head back to work and can't have our phones on the flight line. What time is it there? Are you going to sleep?

My eyes darted to the clock on my bedside.

Me: It's after 10, so yes, I definitely need to sleep. Gotta wake up at 5:30.

Jake: That's around dinner time for me. I'll be around if you want to chat.

Me: Sounds good.

Jake: Sweet dreams.

The smile on my face was wide enough to make my cheeks hurt. I was in trouble. Big trouble. Or at least I would be if Travis found out.

Two weeks later, I was still grinning from ear to ear after getting "sweet dreams" messages from Jake before bed every night. We'd slipped into an easy routine of communicating twice a day when it worked best for the time difference. We kept it to covert messages, since we hadn't come clean with Travis or my friends. We chatted when he was on his lunch break and I was going to bed and again after he ate dinner when I was waking up.

There was something effortless about the way we got along. He asked open-ended questions that made me feel like he cared about getting to know me. He wanted to know real things ... not my favorite color or type of music. He was curious about how I became a teacher, what I liked to do to relax after a long day, and the number one thing on my bucket list.

I hated comparing Jake to Cory, but when you grow up with someone, you don't ask questions in the same way because you already feel like you know the other person. I liked getting to know Jake. Every day, I woke up excited to talk to him. When my phone made the familiar chime that signaled a message on the Connect app, I had a physical reaction to it. A tingling shot up my spine and back down to my toes. I was just as addicted to messaging Jake after two weeks as I had been that first night I'd fallen asleep with him on my mind.

We still hadn't video chatted, though we'd talked about it a couple of times. I looked around my empty classroom and checked the time on my watch. My students wouldn't be there for another forty minutes, and I'd already finished all of the prep work that needed to be done for the day. I quickly calculated that it was about ten o'clock at night in Japan. Would he still be awake? I pulled out my phone and opened a message.

Me: You up?

Jake: Yep.

Me: So ... my kids won't be here for a little while. I was thinking maybe we could video chat?

I held my breath and waited for his response. There

was a pause, and I wondered if I'd messed up. Was that taking things too far? I looked at the ceiling as the seconds ticked by without a response from him. Then, to my surprise, a message came through with only his phone number. He wanted me to video call him.

I swallowed hard, deciding to ask for confirmation that he was ready before I called the number just in case my brother was around. I didn't think Jake would be that careless, but still. We'd done a good job of keeping our conversations between us for the last two weeks, and I didn't want to ruin it now.

Me: Now?

Jake: Yep, I came outside.

I took a makeup bag out of my desk drawer, pulled out my compact, and quickly checked my appearance in the small mirror. Satisfied, I put the bag away and shook my arms to get the jitters out. This seriously felt like a first date. It wasn't, of course, because we were still just friends. But it felt like one.

With shaky fingers, I made the call.

"Hey," Jake said when our video call connected. His smile was wide and his blue eyes were visible even in the dim light of the streetlight nearby.

"Hi," I said, the word coming out all breathy. I hoped I didn't sound as nervous as I felt. "How are you?"

"Great. It's really great to see you."

I blushed. "You too."

"So," he began, laughing a little. "Sorry, this is ..."

"A little weird?" I finished for him.

"No, not weird. Do you think it's weird?"

I shook my head and chuckled. "Not weird, sorry. I'm just ..."

"Nervous?" he asked.

My cheeks were already hurting from smiling. "You too?"

"Yeah."

"Well, I'm glad we're getting it out of the way, then. It's so crazy that it's dark out for you," I observed, glancing around my sunlit classroom.

"Yeah, it's pretty late. Your brother had just gone to sleep when I left."

I bit my lip, and saw his eyes dart down as if he looked at it, then back up to meet my eyes. A warm feeling spread through me. Was this attraction? It was so foreign and strange for me to be attracted to a guy on the other end of a phone. A guy I'd literally only see photos of before this moment. And yet, from half a world away and on the other side of an LCD screen, I felt warmth between us. Who were we kidding? There was more than friendship between us. But the question was, could we act on it?

"I have to ask," I said, clearing my throat. "Does Travis ever ask who you're always talking to?"

He laughed. "I keep telling him and my other two buddies that it's different girls. I don't want them to get all curious about why I'd be talking to one girl so much."

"And why are you talking to one girl so much?" It was a hard flirt. I knew it. He knew it. But as soon as I'd seen those eyes in real life (sort of) all bets were off with the friend thing.

"I'm not sure," he replied. "But it probably makes me pretty insane considering who you are. Do your friends know you're talking to me or do they still think you're always talking to Robby?"

Hearing him bring up my lie about poor Robby gave me a jolt of guilt. Rachel had been strictly against me talking to Jake and potentially causing drama with Travis again. She'd been pretty insistent that I let it go. Nora was a little less opposed to the whole thing, but I couldn't tell her about Jake and not tell Rachel. I sort of tried to tell them both about him at first, but then, just couldn't. After a few days, I told them I was talking to Robby whenever I was talking to Jake. Usually they weren't around when we talked since it was either early in the morning or late at night, so that helped.

I wrinkled my nose. "I haven't fessed up yet. I probably should, though."

"Eh," Jake shrugged. "It's nobody's business."

"Right."

"We're heading to Korea tomorrow," he said.

I sat up a little straighter. "Really? How long will you be there?"

"A couple weeks. Then it's Hawaii for a week."

"Jealous."

"You should come out and visit," he said, a twinkle in his gorgeous blue eyes.

My heart picked up speed. "To Hawaii?"

"Yeah, why not?"

"Is that a thing? Visiting people while they're on deployment?"

Jake shrugged. "We'll probably be pretty busy, and it's only a week. But it would be cool to see you in real life."

"It would be," I said, looking at the calendar on my desk, calculating the weeks. I frowned back at him. "You'll be in Hawaii the week before my spring break. I was definitely tempted."

"Bummer."

"Anyway, remember that kid I was telling you about who broke his arm when he jumped off the playground equipment?"

Jake chuckled. "Yeah, the one who said he was jumping out of a helicopter into enemy territory?"

"The one and only. He knows my brother is a Marine and asked if he could come in to talk to the class about being in the military. I was thinking about asking

Trav if he'll do a video chat with them since he can't physically be here."

"That's a great idea."

"Thanks, but you know Trav, he'll probably try to blow me off. He gets all embarrassed about that kind of thing. Think you can help me convince him to do it? And maybe you and your other friends could make an appearance? The kids would love it."

Jake narrowed his eyes at me but his lips twitched like he was holding back a grin. "I see what Brooks meant about you."

I scowled. "What?"

"He made a comment once about his sister always getting whatever she wants. I get it. Does anyone ever say no to you?"

"Rarely," I said with a slow smile. "Does this mean you'll help?"

"Of course," he replied.

"Thank you." It occurred to me that I didn't know anything about Jake's family. "Hey, do you have a sister? A brother? We haven't talked about your family."

An unmistakable shadow crossed over his features. Even in the dim light I saw his eyes darken and his posture stiffen.

He scratched his nose and stared over the top of the phone. "Uh ..."

"We don't have to talk about it," I said quickly.

"No, it's okay. I just don't really talk about them much."

I swallowed. I really wanted to know his story. We'd talked a lot about his present over the last two weeks. I knew all about his hobbies and his life in the Marines. I knew a little bit about his future plans in Fort Worth and that he was nervous to transition out of the Marine Corps. In fact, he'd mentioned how much the Marines had given him. I wondered if that meant he hadn't had much to begin with ... Was it was too soon to expect him to open up about his past?

"I have an older brother," Jake said after a minute. "He's in prison. Or at least, he was. I haven't talked to him in a long time."

I nodded once. "I see."

"Are you weirded out now? I don't usually lead with the convict brother thing, you know?"

"I'm not weirded out," I said, laughing slightly. "Thank you for telling me. And we don't have to keep talking about it right now."

"You look really pretty today, by the way. Or I guess, you look really pretty, in general, since this is the first time I've seen you outside of pictures. I'm glad you suggested this."

I blushed, then covered one of my cheeks with my hand. "Me too. And thank you."

"Aren't you going to say I'm really pretty, too?" He

put a hand on his chest like he was wounded, making us both laugh, which lightened the moment.

"I wasn't sure what I expected. Talking on the phone, that is," I admitted. "I was nervous. I thought it would be different from talking to you on the app."

"I think it's pretty different. I like being able to look at you."

I narrowed my eyes at him. "You're a flirt."

"So are you."

I snorted. "I didn't used to be."

He pursed his lips. "Speaking of ..."

I didn't answer, just made an expression that signaled for him to go on.

"I kind of already know about your ex," he finished. "I've been meaning to tell you, but there hasn't been a good time."

Sighing heavily, I looked around my empty classroom. I wasn't sure if I was ready to talk about Cory with Jake. But I was curious about what he already knew from Travis. Besides, I'd asked him to reveal something personal about himself, and he had. I was sure it hadn't been easy and I was grateful he'd done it. I supposed it was only right for me to open up, too.

"Did I mess up?" he asked, trying to read into my silence.

I shook my head. "No, we should talk about it. You

told me about your brother. So, we might as well talk about my ex."

Jake laughed. "Getting to the hard stuff now. It can't all be rainbows and butterflies."

"Exactly. Plus ... talking about my ex does have a little bit to do with ... this."

He pursed his lips. "Yep. I can see that."

"What did Travis tell you?"

Jake scratched the back of his neck and shifted in his seat. "We've had a few conversations about it. Basically, I know you were with the guy—Cory, right?— since you guys were all in middle school. And he was Brooks's best friend."

"Mm-hmm."

"And Brooks said it took him a long time to be cool with you two dating, but once he was cool with it, he supported you guys all the way."

I nodded. "Yep."

His jaw clenched. "And then last year you thought he was taking you out on some romantic dinner to propose, but instead he told you he was leaving."

It had been long enough that I thought I could talk about it without having a physical reaction to the pain of that night. Based on the tingling in my fingers, I wasn't completely healed. Or maybe it was just hearing Jake repeat it all back to me. This new happiness collided with that low point in my life, resulting in a sick feeling in my stomach.

I still remembered how long I'd spent getting ready that night. I'd taken care to make sure my dress, nails, hair, makeup, and shoes all looked perfect for the occasion. Cory had told me in advance where we were going and that he had something important to discuss with me. When I'd said it was too much—too fancy for a firefighter and a teacher—he'd insisted that I deserved it. That was what had convinced me it was the night I'd get engaged.

My friends and I had spent hours going over every detail. We'd talked about what to order so I didn't have spinach in my teeth when I smiled. We'd joked about different ways to say yes to the big question. We'd even concocted a plan for them to be at the restaurant so they could hide nearby to take pictures of him proposing. Cory wouldn't have thought to have someone record it, of course. We'd figured after it happened, he'd be grateful for their stakeout because it meant we'd have a keepsake of one of the happiest nights of our lives. Instead, I'd been the one who was grateful, since it meant my best friends were there to take me home after he'd humiliated me by dumping me in public.

I shook my head to clear the memories away. "Yep."

"And the reason Brooks hates him—aside from the fact that any brother would hate the guy who broke his sister's heart—is because he didn't even tell him where his head was at. He just left."

"He took off and left my brother to pick up the pieces," I added. "My mom was the one who told Travis what happened. I couldn't."

"I'm sorry, Ivy."

I gave him a sad smile. "It's okay. I've accepted that it's for the best. But as far as Travis goes, things were kind of strained, I guess, for a while."

"I bet."

"We're finally back on track and talking more. But that's why this whole thing with you makes me nervous. I swear, deep down, Travis blames me for him and Cory not being friends anymore."

He hung his head, then looked back up at me. "I know firsthand how mad he was about Cory. But, if it helps, he never said he was mad at you. It was always Cory's fault for leaving the way he did."

"Thank you. I appreciate that."

"And, yeah ... he was also mad about him hurting you. He's protective, that's for sure."

"And that makes me feel even more guilty for talking to you." I couldn't meet his eyes.

Jake sighed. "It was almost easier to just message on the app. This—talking face-to-face—is much worse as far as the level of treason."

"I agree," I said, putting my free hand on my cheek,

feeling the warmth of another blush underneath my palm. "What do we do?"

He hesitated. "The safest thing would be to cut it off right here. Stop talking now, and we can honestly say we spent a couple weeks talking about Fort Worth and just being friendly."

Rocks settled in my belly. "Yeah and then, of course, I'll be here if you need anything after you move."

"Which is what Brooks wants. He told me his family would be like my family."

We kind of looked at each other then, the awkwardness of that comment—considering our mutual attraction—made both of us laugh.

"I have to go," I said, looking at the time. "My kids will be here soon."

"Well, I guess we'll have to talk again later, just to see if we should keep talking."

I nodded. "Right. That will definitely require another conversation."

"Have a good day, teach," he said with a wink that absolutely melted me.

As I hung up and smoothed my hands over my skirt to collect myself, I knew one thing for sure. It was bad that I had spent the last two weeks getting to know my brother's best friend on a dating app ... but it was way worse now that I'd talked to him (almost) face-to-face.

6

JAKE

Ivy: You're invited to a wedding. Do you choose chicken or beef?

Me: Easy. Beef. You?

Ivy: Beef. Texas, duh. But also ... I'm picky about chicken.

Me: Are you a boneless wing kinda girl?

Ivy: Actually, I'm a dip-my-pizza-in-the-buffalo-sauce-but-skip-the-wings kinda girl.

I smiled. Talking to Ivy got easier every day. We kept it light. Casual. Fun. She was a welcome source of warmth in my life, taking my mind off long days spent in the cold winter air in Korea. In addition to texting twice a day, for the last week we'd also been video chatting every night after Brooks went to sleep. We'd had a couple close calls where he'd woken up and texted me to ask where I was. It was easy enough to tell him I'd been using the bathroom, but he was starting to make jokes about my nightly bathroom trips.

Ivy: Speaking of food, what's for lunch at the chow hall today?

Me: Meatloaf. Your brother is complaining about it. Says it's not as good as his mom's.

Ivy: LOL. She makes a good meatloaf. You'll have to come for dinner sometime when you move here.

Me: That sounds like a bad idea.

Ivy: Travis told our mom to take care of you when you get here. Including family dinners.

Me: If you told your mom about us talking, how do you think she'd react?

Ivy: Hmm ...

Me: Not well?

I held my breath as I waited for her answer. A few days earlier we'd officially stopped pretending we weren't into each other. It was pointless. We had one, maybe two, conversations about how we probably shouldn't talk anymore because of Brooks, but then we just ... didn't stop.

Ivy: After everything with Cory went down, I could tell it upset her that both of her kids were hurt by the whole thing. I guess she'd be wary of that

happening again. I'm worried about it, too, if I'm being honest.

My stomach turned and I stared at my half-eaten lunch. I wasn't hungry anymore. Yes, talking to Ivy was great … as long as we didn't wade into these touchy waters. When that happened, and the guilt hit us both, it got weird.

Me: It won't happen again. Trust me. I already told you I don't like big cities.

Ivy: You know that's not what I meant.

I knew. But I tried for humor to deflect it.

Me: Let's try not to think about that kind of stuff right now. It's only the beginning.

Ivy: Okay. You're right.

"Any winners?" Brooks asked, nodding at the phone in my hand.

I looked down at the incriminating texts between me and Ivy. We'd moved off the dating app and over to regular texting, and I'd saved her number in my phone as "Texas." I'd been too freaked out about messaging her in Connect with her actual first name and photo, just in case Brooks ever saw it. Did it feel sneaky? One hundred percent. Did I feel bad about it? Sure. Did I want to stop talking to Ivy? No freaking way.

"A few, yeah," I said with a shrug.

Brooks grinned and tipped his imaginary cowboy hat at me. "See? What did I tell you? Texas girls, man."

"You weren't lying."

"Heck no, I wasn't," he gestured for the phone. "Lemme see if I know anyone. It's not that small of a town, but you never know."

I froze. It was smaller than he knew. I hadn't talked to anyone on the app since Ivy and I had moved over to texts. I couldn't show him any recent conversations with anyone other than his sister, but I still had some connections I could show him. One thing was for sure —I'd need to handle this very carefully and not let him have free rein over my phone.

"Hang on," I said, opening Connect and pulling up a picture of a pretty blonde I'd made a connection with when I'd first switched my settings over to Fort Worth. I turned the phone toward him. "Her name's Jill. She's a hair stylist."

Brooks squinted at the pic, then shook his head. "Don't know her. Next."

I breathed out a sigh of relief that he was only interested in taking a quick look and not asking more questions or digging deeper. I pulled up another profile and showed him the pic. "Do you know Amberlee?"

"Amberlee? Now, that's a Texas name for ya," he said, looking at the pic. "But no, I don't know her either."

"How about Katie?" I asked, showing him a third pic.

He looked, then shook his head. "Man, I'm oh for three. I was hoping I'd know one of these girls so I could warn her about you."

"Yeah, yeah," I said, relieved to be able to put my phone safely in my pocket.

Brooks sighed. "Well, maybe Fort Worth is bigger than I thought."

I chuckled and scratched my forehead. Oh, the irony.

"Speaking of Texas," Brooks said, tossing his wadded up napkin on top of his now empty plate and pushing it away. "My sister—she's a teacher, remember? —wants me to do some kind of career day type thing for her class."

I rubbed my palms on my thighs. I was supposed to get him to say yes to this proposal without letting on that I knew anything about it, and the pressure was on. "Oh, yeah?"

"Yeah," he grimaced.

"I take it you don't want to do it?"

He shook his head. "Does that make me a huge jerk? I mean, they're little kids. Last deployment, I got shot. How am I supposed to talk to a bunch of kids about getting shot?"

I swallowed. I'd been on that deployment with him, but I wasn't actually with him when he'd gotten shot.

I'd never forget what it was like when Hawk and I heard the news that our friends were injured. It took me back to some really dark days in my life when I'd felt powerless and as though the only thing I could do was wish for something bigger to step in and fix everything. In some ways, that incident changed my life. There'd been a chapel on the ship, and some of the guys went there to pray for our guys in Kandahar. I hadn't stopped finding reasons to pray ever since. I only wished I'd known that kind of comfort when I was a kid, too.

I blew out a breath and came back to the task at hand. "Well, I wouldn't lead with that."

"Bro, I'm serious," Brooks said. "How do I tell her no without getting her all mad at me?"

"I don't think you should say no," I said simply.

He let his head fall back in exasperation. "Wrong answer."

"You don't have to tell them about getting shot. There's plenty of stuff you can talk to them about."

"Murph, everything we do seems so ... violent. Think about it. Even though we're out here in the Pacific instead of the Middle East, we still load bombs on jets. Those jets take off, and drop the bombs. That's pretty heavy stuff. They're like five years old."

I shrugged. "That's my point. They have no concept of violence. They see us as heroes, man. Their parents tell them we're out here fighting the bad guys and keeping America safe. You can work with that."

He picked at the edge of his sleeve. "I don't know how long I can talk about generic stuff like that without running out of things to say. That could get awkward."

"Why don't we all do it together? Me, you, Mills, and Hawk? I'm sure between the four of us we can make it funny or whatever. The kids'll love it."

Brooks considered my idea. "Hmm. I like it. Takes the pressure off of me, that's for sure."

Victory. I couldn't help but smile at the fact that I was able to help convince him to do the video call with Ivy's class. "I'm sure Iv — I mean, your sister will be glad you said yes."

"Yeah," he agreed, not thinking twice about my stuttering. "I guess she will. We haven't talked much lately, so it was cool of her to ask me to do it."

I poked at my food but didn't reply.

"We didn't used to need a reason to talk," Brooks continued, "but everything has been so messed up since my loser friend skipped out on her. Man, I never should have let that go on for as long as it did."

I grimaced and looked away. Before I started talking to Ivy, I never thought anything of it when Brooks talked to me about his sister and her ex-boyfriend. I didn't mind being an ear for him to vent to about something that clearly bothered him. Talking about it now had me feeling all sorts of slimy.

"Well," I said, choosing my words carefully, "it's not like you really could have stopped it right? If they were ... in love. Or whatever."

Man, this was awkward.

"We were kids when they started all of that. I probably could have told Cory I wouldn't be friends with him anymore if he dated my sister, and he probably wouldn't have been man enough to stand up to me at that age. You know? I could've saved us all a lot of heartbreak if I'd have just nipped it in the bud."

Heat prickled up the back of my neck. "Mm-hmm."

"I mean, it's not like I blame *her* for what happened with Cory, you know?" Brooks continued.

I rubbed the back of my neck. "For sure."

"I blame myself. They just seemed so good together. And they were happy. And I cared about both of them. Who was I to get in the way of all that?"

My mind was spinning. Would he want to nip this in the bud? Or would he not want to get in the way of our happiness since he cared about us both? If I was honest with him now, I could find out before things got past the point of no return.

"Can I tell you something, though?" he asked, leaning forward.

"Go for it."

"If they ever got back together, I'd probably punch him out. No lie."

I gulped. I think I'll just keep my mouth shut, after all.

7

IVY

"Okay, everyone," I said to my room full of kindergartners, "grab your drawings and come sit on the carpet. It's almost time."

Giggles and chatter filled the air as the children hurried from their seats and over to the colorful rug in front of the white board. They couldn't contain their excitement, and peppered me with questions as I lowered the projection screen over the sight words we'd been working on that day.

"Relax, you'll get to ask the Marines your questions soon," I told them, beaming at their sweet faces. "No, Hannah, they're not going to be here in real life, they're far away. You'll see, hang in there."

I set my laptop up in front of the rug so that the kids could be seen in the front facing camera, then crouched down in front of it to start the video call with my brother. He answered it, his brows knit together in a scowl while he looked for the button to unmute himself. When he found it, the scowl dissolved into a grin.

"Hey, Vee," he said, with a small wave.

"Hey," I replied. "Thanks again for doing this! The kids have been looking forward to this all week! Hang on, let me put you on the board in front of the class."

"Cool."

While I clicked around to set up the projection, I noticed him push the computer back further on the picnic table in front of him. Two more Marines came into view, causing my breath to catch as I searched their faces to see if one of them was Jake. Disappointment coursed through me when I realized that neither of the men in uniform next to my brother was my secret … friend.

"Is this everyone?" I asked, trying hard to keep my voice even and unattached, though my eyes darted around the screen looking for Jake.

"Yeah," Travis said. "Oh, wait, no. Hawk, is Murphy coming?"

The Marine to the left of Travis looked at his watch. "He said he would. I'll text him."

"It's okay," I said, feigning lack of interest as Hawk

pushed buttons on his phone. "This is great. Thanks for coming, you guys."

"Anything for you, sis," Travis said, making a sarcastic face at me.

I pushed the button on the display settings on my screen and the Marines appeared, larger than life, in front of my class. A cheer rang out from the rambunctious kids, which made the guys smile. The kids waved and hollered and several of them forgot they were supposed to be sitting down and jumped high in the air.

I clapped my hands and addressed the class. "One, two, three, eyes on me."

The class settled down as much as they could, and the Marines laughed, waiting for me to lead the discussion.

"Everyone," I began, "this guy here in the middle is my big brother, Travis."

"Ms. Brooks, it says Brooks right there," one of my students said, jumping up and hitting the screen where Travis's name tag was.

"Yep, sit down, John," I said, laughing. "That's because his last name is Brooks, too."

"Because you're not married to anyone?" another student asked.

"That's right, Kevin," I said.

Just then, Jake jumped up from behind the other guys and yelled, "Boo!"

The class—and the Marines—jumped and then laughed. I put a hand over my heart and exhaled sharply. "These are my brother's friends, class."

The class shouted their hellos, and I fought off the urge to introduce the Marines by name. Yes, Jake had given me quite the rundown on his friends over the last few weeks, so I felt like I knew them well. But as far as my brother was concerned, I hardly knew them at all. Especially Jake.

"Trav, will you introduce your friends?" I asked.

Travis nodded and put his arms around his friends. "Yeah, this here is my buddy Hawk."

"Like the bird?" one of the kids called out.

Hawk flapped his arms like wings and made a *caw, caw* noise, making the kids laugh.

"His last name is Hawkins, so it's a nickname," Travis answered, swatting one of Hawk's long arms out of his personal space. "And this guy over here is Mills."

"But you can call me Matt," his buddy interjected.

"Hi, Matt," the kids wailed.

I held my breath as the guys situated themselves so Jake could be seen in the screen. He looked so freaking good in his cammies, I couldn't even handle it. Our video calls were always after he'd already showered and changed over to his civilian clothes at the end of the day, so I'd never actually seen him in uniform before. I rolled my shoulders and tried to keep myself from swooning in front of my class—and my brother.

"And this scary guy is Jake Murphy," Travis finished up his introduction.

Jake waved at the class and they waved in return, yelling their hellos.

"Thank you for coming," I said to the guys, then turned to my class. "Kids, do you want to show these Marines your drawings?"

The class cheered, and again, some of the more rambunctious students jumped up from their seated positions and tried to get in front of the other kids. I called out to them to sit back down and for the rest of the class to hush so we could talk to our friends on the screen.

"Those drawings are great," Travis said, he and the other guys leaning forward to get a better look. "And we liked the ones you sent us in the mail, too."

The kids nearly lost their minds when Travis held up the cards the class had made for them over a month earlier. I nodded my head in encouragement when they looked back at me, surprised their cards had actually made it across the world.

"Why is it dark outside?" one of my students asked.

"Because we're really far away, and where we are, it's already almost midnight," Hawk answered, his eyes wide, knowing how late that is to a kid.

I was grateful to my brother and his friends for staying up late so we could do this. I'd planned it for first thing in the morning after announcements so they wouldn't have to stay up too terribly late. And I was especially grateful that they'd agreed to stay in their uniforms for the call, knowing how important visuals like that were for five-year-olds. We couldn't have them looking like regular guys in T-shirts, even though that's what they were. They had to look the part of the Marine or I'd get a million complaints from these kids.

"Do you guys have any other questions for the Marines?" I prompted the class. "Raise your hands. Yes, Joey. Go ahead."

"My mom said you guys are superheroes. Do you have any powers?" Joey asked, his face skeptical.

The Marines nodded seriously and looked at one another, obviously working on their answer.

"Yeah," Travis answered. "Of course, we do."

"Like what?" a few kids prompted them. "What powers?"

"Do you have a Top Secret security clearance?" Matt asked.

"No!" the class shouted back.

"Well, then I'm sorry, we can't tell you about our powers," Jake said with a wink that made a smile spread reflexively across my face. It seemed like he was looking right at me, but I knew that wasn't the case.

"Aw," the class whined.

I stepped up. "Don't worry, friends, these guys might not be able to tell you their powers, but I can. They are all very ... brave. That's one of their main superpowers. They run towards danger instead of away. And they protect us and fight for us so that we are safe here in America."

The Marines on the screen smiled the typically modest smiles that I knew they would, but some of the kids in my class weren't impressed.

"I meant powers like ... can they fly?" Joey clarified.

Everyone laughed, and Travis shook his head. "No, sorry, bud. But we do get to work on F-18s. Do you know what those are?"

A couple kids said, "Jets," which I could tell Travis and his friends loved. I'd shown them pictures of the jets my brother worked on back when we'd made the cards to send to him, and I was proud of them for remembering. Plus, we had a couple of military kids whose parents worked on the Joint Reserve Base where Jake would soon be working. I couldn't help but notice Jake's reaction to my kids. He nodded and smiled as if he were impressed with them, and I stood a little straighter. They were the best.

"Exactly," Hawk said. "Jets. We get to load bombs—"

Travis swatted Hawk on the chest. "Ixnay on the ombsbay, man."

I giggled, grateful to my brother for putting a stop to that line of discussion. Even if he did use Pig Latin. Such a dork.

Jake cleared his throat and leaned in. "Does anyone else have any questions?"

"How do you become a Marine?" one of my quietest students asked, surprising me.

"First, you go to a recruiting office. Then, you sign up, and they send you to boot camp," Matt answered.

"That's where I met this guy right here," Hawk added, reaching across Travis and patting Matt on the shoulder. "Now we're best friends."

"What do you do in boot camp?" another kid asked.

"You climb to the top of super-tall walls using ropes," Jake answered. "And you crawl through mud."

"And you have to eat really, really fast," Travis added, making me laugh because I knew how much time it had taken for him to revert back to eating at a normal speed after he'd graduated boot camp.

"Do you get yelled at a lot?" John asked, wrinkling his nose.

"Yes," all four Marines said in unison.

"You also practice marching," Jake said. "Can you guys march?"

Limbs flew in all directions as my class jumped to their feet and began marching around. They zigged, zagged, ran into each other, and fell over laughing. I wasn't sure what Jake thought was going to happen when he asked the kids if they could march. Did he think they'd use their voices to answer instead of their bodies? He had a lot to learn about kindergartners, if so.

It took me a few attempts, but I finally got them settled down and asking more and more questions. The guys were knocking it out of the park, giving examples five-year-olds could understand and appreciate. This was going to go down as one of my favorite days I'd ever had as a teacher.

"Any other questions?" Travis asked.

The students all shouted their questions at once, causing me to step in and regulate the conversation a little bit. Twenty minutes, and what felt like fifty questions later, we were losing them to their excitement and lack of focus. Even though I was met with lots of sadness over it, I called for the last question.

"Go ahead, Sara," I pointed at one of my students who hadn't gotten to ask a question yet, shaking my head at all of the sounds of disappointment coming from the other kids who'd asked more questions. "I know it's sad to say goodbye to our friends. But we can't take up too much of their time. Remember, it's the middle of the night where they are. Sara, what's your question?"

"Do you love being a Marine?"

Without hesitation, all four of them sat up a little straighter and smiled.

"Absolutely," Travis said, his friends nodding in agreement.

"It's the best job ever," Hawk said. "But this guy, here, is going to stop being a Marine in a few months. Right, Murph?"

Travis cut in. "Hey, kids, our buddy Jake is going to move to Fort Worth and work on jets at the JRB base."

The kids got all excited. It must have delighted them to hear of some connection between these heroes and the town they lived in.

"Will you come see us?" one of the kids asked.

"Maybe your teacher can bring him in to see you guys sometime," Travis suggested, apparently forgetting they'd be on summer break and not my class anymore by the time Jake moved to Fort Worth.

Quickly, I did what any good teacher would do in that situation and pulled out the ever popular, noncommittal, "We'll see."

The kids cheered, poor things, and I made a face at Travis as if to say, Nice job, genius. Jake smirked in the background. I wondered if he was thinking about how funny it was that his best friend was setting up reasons for us to hang out once he moved to Fort Worth. I couldn't help it, that was something I seriously looked forward to.

8

JAKE

F resh from my shower, I threw myself onto the queen-size hotel bed, face-first into my pillow. I groaned. My entire body was sore. We'd loaded over twenty bombs onto a dozen jets, each one weighing around five hundred pounds. If I wasn't too tired to blink, I'd be grateful for the ten thousand pound workout.

"I'm dead," Hawk said from the chaise lounge against the window. "I thought Korea was supposed to be an easier workload than Japan."

Brooks was my roommate at the hotel in South Korea where we'd been staying for the past week, and he chuckled from the other queen-size bed next to mine. "Ah, come on. It wasn't that bad."

"Bro," Mills yelled from his bed in the adjoining

room. "It wasn't bad for you because you're the Jolly Green freaking Giant. Don't rub it in."

I snorted into my pillow. Mills wasn't wrong. Brooks was like six and a half feet tall and looked like he ate five-hundred pound bombs for breakfast. I was just glad to have him out on the line when we were working, seeing as how he could lift as much as two of our newbie lance corporals could. I could hold my own, but I was out of practice with loading bombs since there was plenty of paper pushing that needed to get done, too.

A knock sounded at our door, so I turned my head to the side and opened one eye. "Not it."

"Man, I'm disappointed in you," Brooks said with a shake of his head as he easily got up and headed for the door.

He came back with the classic white-and-red Priority Mail shipping box that care packages always showed up in. No one had ever sent me a care package, so I turned my head back to the window.

"I bet my sister sent me some more stuff," Brooks said.

I turned back toward him, curious, despite myself. I was sure that even if that package was from Ivy, there wouldn't be anything in it for me. But still. If it came from her, I kind of wanted to see what it was.

"Wait a minute," Brooks said. "This isn't even for me."

"Who's it for?" I asked, popping my head up, nerves swirling at the possibility of Brooks holding a package his sister had sent for his best friend instead of him.

"Mills," he called to our buddy in the other room. "They brought your package to our door."

My head dropped back down on the pillow, and I tried to ignore the feeling of disappointment that coursed through me. Of course Ivy wouldn't risk Brooks finding out about us by sending me something. It was dumb of me to even think that.

Mills came through the doorway between our two rooms and rubbed his hands together. "Man, the wife said she mailed this like two weeks ago. I didn't think it would take that long to get here."

"What is it?" Hawk asked.

"I don't know, but she's been bugging me about it every day this week," Mills replied, using his pocketknife to slice open the tape on the box. His eyes lit up as he opened the flaps. "Sweet. We got some jerky, energy drink mix, candy ...."

"Liv knows the way to your heart is through your gut," Brooks commented, sitting down on the bed and leaning back against the headboard.

"Very funny. There's also a couple books, because I'm not just a dumb cowboy like you," Mills jabbed, still unpacking the box onto the bed. "Oh look, some protein powder."

"There we go," Brooks chuckled.

"What's this? A T-shirt?" He picked up a black roll of fabric, unrolled it, and held it up against his chest. As he did, a smaller piece of black fabric fell onto the floor at his feet. He looked down at the shirt, and the object that fell, but didn't say a word.

It took my mind a minute to catch up to the words on the shirt. There were stars and lightning bolts surrounding the text, which read, Every Superhero Needs a Sidekick. I lifted up on my elbows and leaned over the edge of the bed, my eyes landing on the thing that fell. It was a matching onesie, the words reading, I'm the Sidekick.

Brooks was reading the shirt and the onesie, his mouth hanging open, his eyes darting between me and Mills. I turned my head to look at Hawk, who'd fallen asleep in the chair somewhere between the beef jerky and the figurative bomb that just went off in the center of the hotel room.

I grabbed my pillow and threw it at Hawk. "What's going on?" he jumped.

"Mills is gonna be a daddy," Brooks yelled, a huge grin spread across his face. He stood from the bed and scooped up the onesie, holding it up against his broad chest. "It's so small. Man, congratulations."

Mills had no expression on his face, which was white as a ghost. He stared at the onesie that Brooks still displayed against him, then looked back at the matching shirt he held. I glanced at Hawk, who had leaned forward in his seat and rested his chin on his steepled hands. He was watching Mills like a ... well, like a hawk.

After Mills had been shot on the last deployment, he'd suffered from a bad case of PTSD. He'd had nightmares, hallucinations, panic attacks, and more. He'd even left Olivia because he was scared that he'd lash out and hurt her. They'd eventually gotten back together, but not before six months of counseling and a scheme from Hawk and his wife to force them to spend a week in a cabin together.

Since then, he'd pretty much had his PTSD symptoms under control. Where he used to freak out and rage anytime he found himself in a stressful situation, he now would breathe and count to ten or whatever coping strategy his doctor helped him develop. Still, at the end of the day, we all knew how much Mills hated the lack of control that came from his PTSD.

"You okay, Mills?" I asked evenly, careful not to make any moves that would startle him, just in case.

Mills looked at me, but didn't reply.

Hawk cleared his throat. "Mills, does Olivia know you don't want kids, man?"

Brooks made a face at Hawk, then looked at me. I shrugged. It was news to me. Mills must have only told Hawk about his feelings on the kid thing.

"No," Mills said. "I mean, not really. Every time she brought it up I kind of just … changed the subject."

Brooks's eyes bulged out of his head. "Are you serious? You don't want kids?"

"No, dude," Mills snapped.

"Why not?" Brooks asked.

Mills sighed. "Brooks, I know you were there, but you don't get it. You had a bad flesh wound, but I got messed up in the head. I don't want a kid to be around that."

I felt my chest tightened as my friend's words hit home. He was going to be a great dad simply because he cared about what kind of life his kid would have. My own father had never thought twice about what kind of environment his sons lived in. And it had been nowhere close to a good one.

Brooks rolled his eyes. "Look, man, I support your recovery or whatever, but you're fine. You're better than fine. Look at you. You get through stressful situations without missing a beat now, man."

I cleared my throat. "How long has it been since you had one of your dreams or hallucinations?"

"The dreams are still pretty frequent." Mills

shrugged. "But the hallucinations are gone for the most part."

Hawk nodded. "Well, that was the biggest reason why you didn't want to be with Liv, right? That was the scariest part—not knowing what was real when you were awake. If that part is gone, maybe the kid thing isn't so bad?"

Mills looked in the box. I wasn't sure what else he expected to find in there, but he took out a couple more snacks and some magazines, then his shoulders sagged as he looked at whatever was left inside. He picked up the box and held it up to us, showing us what was written on the bottom of the box. There was an ultrasound picture taped to the center with Baby Mills Coming this Fall written on it.

Hawk stepped forward and pulled the ultrasound picture off the box, squinting at it. "Doing some date checking here, sorry not sorry."

Brooks and I groaned and shot him dirty looks, and Mills said, "Seriously, Spencer?"

"It says she's six weeks and four days on this pic. And she mailed this box like two weeks ago, right? So, she'd be almost nine weeks now." Hawk counted on his fingers. "Looks like this happened what, like, right before we left?"

"I guess," Mills shrugged.

"Then it adds up," Hawk decided, handing Mills the photo.

"Gee, thanks, bud," Mills said sardonically. "Because *that's* what I'm worried about."

Hawk held out his hands. "Hey, man, just making sure. We're on deployment after all."

"Okay," I got up from the bed and grabbed Mills by the shoulder. "Listen, Mills. This is going to be cool. You're going to be a great dad. Liv has probably been super excited for you to get this package, so you need to snap out of it and be happy when you call her to say you got it."

Brooks tossed the onesie at Mills. "It's going to be more than cool. It's going to be awesome. I can't wait to be a dad. I want a son first, and then a daughter. Like my parents had. One of each, so I can do all the cool dad stuff with each of them. Camping and scouts with my boy. I'll teach him how to shoot beer cans in the desert and fish on the lake. And the girl—man, I can't wait to do all that daddy-daughter stuff and threaten her boyfriends. It's gonna be great."

Mills shook his head. "You've given this a lot of thought."

"Yeah, tons," Brooks continued. "And I want the boy to be an awesome big brother like I was. He'll always be there to protect her and keep bullies away. I'll need to teach him to keep his friends away from her, though. I messed up there, and it didn't turn out well."

I gulped and backed up, sitting down on the bed. That was not easy to hear, given my current secret life talking to his sister every chance I got. Hawk caught my eye and made a face at me, and I glared back at him. Did he know something about me and Ivy? No, he couldn't. I was being careful. As far as he and Mills knew, I'd stopped talking to her right when I'd found out who she was. Hawk winked and then went back to focusing on the task at hand, causing a rock to settle deep in my gut. He might know something. And if he did, I was going to be in trouble.

Mills busied himself by piling all of his gifts back in the box. "I'm not sure about this, guys. I know I'm better; Liv knows I'm better. But we're also young. Even before the whole attack happened, we always said we'd wait to have kids until we were like thirty."

"You're not that far off," Hawk said with a shrug.

"You know what they say, Mills," Brooks put a hand on his chest. "If you want to make God laugh, you tell Him your plans."

Mills blew out a breath. "I guess I'd better go call her."

"Yeah, video call would be best. And remember—be happy. This is good," I told my friend, giving him two thumbs up.

"Wait a minute," Mills said, zeroing in on Hawk. "Did you know?"

Hawk's eyes grew wide and he put a hand on his chest. "Who, me?"

"Yeah, you." Mills pointed a finger at Hawk. "Your wife is my wife's best friend. And if I've learned anything these last couple years, it's that nobody in this little friend circle keeps anything a secret. In fact, Brooks, your wife is close to Liv, too. Did you know?"

Brooks pointed at me. "At least you don't have to worry about Murphy. He's not seeing anyone in our group."

Hawk choked out a laugh before quickly turning it into a coughing fit instead, confirming my suspicions that he knows I've been talking to Ivy. I made a mental note to confront him about it later.

Brooks held up his hands to Mills. "Anyway, the girls kept a secret for once, Mills. We would have told you if we'd known. Now, go call your wife."

"Wow," Ivy said when I finished telling her about my eventful afternoon with the guys. She blew out a breath, her full lips flattening into a hard line. "Poor Matt. He's too hard on himself."

"You don't even know the half of it," I said, adjusting my grip on my phone.

I peeked through the glass of the sliding door to make sure Brooks's large form was still on the bed, sleeping. I loved my new nightly routine of sitting on the balcony and video chatting with Ivy, the sights and sounds of Korea in the background.

"Do you want kids?" she asked.

My eyes flew back to hers through the screen. "Do I?"

"Yeah."

"Uh," I said, pausing to think. "Yeah. Yes. Someday. Do you?"

Ivy nodded. "Definitely. I love kids."

"Does that mean you want a lot of them?"

"A few, yeah, God willing. Definitely more than one. I loved having a big brother growing up." Her voice trailed off like she'd said something wrong, and I knew she was thinking about the fact that we'd never finished our conversation about my family.

I gulped. "I loved having a big brother, too. When we were kids, he was the best."

The corner of her lip tilted up into a morose smile. "What happened with your brother, Jake?"

There wasn't a good reason not to tell her. I'd never gotten far enough into a relationship with a girl to tell her about my family before. I just didn't want to bring it up. None of the guys knew anything about my family because they hadn't asked, but it wasn't a secret. I was still a little bit worried about how I would feel talking about it after I'd spent so long trying to avoid thinking about it.

"We had kind of a rough home life," I started. "My mom and dad took turns going in and out of jail. There was always people coming and going ... bad people. At first, the only good thing I had in my life was my big brother. But when he got older, he got mean. Started getting into what my parents were doing and stopped wanting to hang out with me. I think he just figured it was the only way to get their attention."

Ivy's eyes welled up like she was trying to keep them from tearing as she listened.

I cleared my throat before I continued. "Anyway, we butted heads a lot when I was a teenager because I didn't want to be like them. He would call me a Goody Two-shoes and all that. I wasn't a Goody Two-shoes. I just didn't think jail sounded very fun."

"That sounds awful. Did you have a teacher or someone else you could go to when it was bad at your house?"

I smiled. "When I was fourteen, I went into a gas station and there was a Marine recruiter in there."

Ivy's body language relaxed, almost like she could

tell it was a turning point in my life and she was comforted by it.

"He asked me how old I was and where I went to school. I lied and said I was seventeen but almost eighteen. He said we could get the paperwork done and I could leave after my birthday."

"He believed you?" Ivy asked, her mouth open in surprise.

"Yep. We made an appointment for the next day and I told him I was serious about joining. Showed up at his office ready to sign paperwork. Then he asked for my ID. One thing led to another and before I knew it, I was pouring my heart out to the guy. Told him all about my worthless parents and my jerk of a brother. Told him I didn't want to be like them, but I didn't know how to get away from them, either."

"Aw," Ivy put her hand over her heart, "I just want to go back in time and hug teenage-you."

I raised a brow. "I wish you could hug adult-me."

"Shush," she said. "Anyway, don't change the subject. What happened after you told him about your family and everything?"

"He took me under his wing, I guess. He'd just gotten on recruiting duty, so he'd be there for the next three years. He let me come to the office every day and help them with random stuff like filing paperwork or getting them lunch. He wasn't allowed to pay me, but they always bought me food and stuff."

"I love that," she crooned.

"When I turned sixteen," I continued, enjoying talking to her about the good part of my past, "I started working out with the other future Marines at the office. I got a paying job bussing tables, though I still appreciated the recruiters for keeping me out of trouble up until that point."

"How did your family react to you spending all of that time with the Marines?" Ivy asked.

I shrugged. "It wasn't good. They didn't like it. I only told them where I was half the time, anyway."

"Did you have to wait all the way until you were eighteen to join?"

"Yeah," I said, pressure settling onto my chest at the memories. "Right before my recruiter left for his next assignment, we took parental consent paperwork to my dad. I was seventeen and figured they'd want me out of their hair anyway."

"He didn't sign it?"

Shaking my head, I looked over my shoulder again to check on Brooks before answering. "I'd been giving them half of my paycheck for my rent. He didn't want to lose that. Looking back, it's absurd. It was only a few hundred bucks a month. What kind of adult needs his kid's money that bad, you know?"

Ivy closed her eyes and exhaled sharply. "I'm sorry."

"I left as soon as I turned eighteen. I didn't need his permission, and I didn't even tell him I was leaving. Took nothing with me but the clothes on my back and haven't talked to any of them since."

"Jake," Ivy said, the word coming out full of emotion, "I'm really glad you met that recruiter that day."

"Me, too. Now that I'm a Christian, I look back and think about how if I'd just gone home after school instead of to that gas station to kill time, I never would have met him. God's plan."

"Amen," she said, with a small smile. "So ... as far as how all of that circles back to whether or not you want kids ... I have to say, I think where we come from has a huge hand in what kind of parents we'll be, if we let it. I think what you went through, and how alone you must have felt even though you were surrounded by people, will make you a great dad."

Warmth spread throughout my chest. "Thanks."

"And I think the same is true for Matt. The fact that he's worried about how his PTSD will affect his family means he'll be a great dad, too."

"I said the same thing," I told her.

"Great minds think alike."

"As for you," I said, wanting to lighten things up a bit, "I think you'll be a great mom someday because

I've seen those kids you hang out with all day. They're *wild*."

"Hey! You better not be talking smack about my kids," she teased.

I held up a hand. "I would never. But seriously, the patience you must have."

"*Psh*, you deal with my brother every day. You can probably figure out where I learned how to be patient."

I snorted, then caught movement out of the corner of my eye. I peered through the glass, finding an empty space where Brooks used to be on the bed. The light was on in the bathroom. If he came out here, there was no way I'd be able hide that I was video chatting with someone, and you'd better believe he'd want to know who it was.

"Speaking of your brother, I should go before he catches us."

"Sweet dreams," she said, giving a small wave before ending the call.

I put my phone in my pocket and leaned my head back against the chair. The glow of the city was hypnotizing. I couldn't believe I'd just told her about all of that. Up until this conversation, she'd known me just as well as her brother knew me. Tonight, we crossed into new territory. She now knew me better than anyone currently in my life. I looked up at the sky and said a prayer that it wouldn't all be for nothing.

9

IVY

"Hey," I said, smiling at my brother through the phone. "I wanted to thank you again for talking to my class the other day."

"No biggie," Travis replied. "It was actually kind of fun. Especially because the guys came on with me. I wouldn't have had a clue what to say to all those kids if I'd been alone."

I nodded. "Oh yeah, the comic relief from Hawkins was great. He's ridiculous."

"You hear that, Hawk?" Travis looked over the top of the phone, presumably at Hawkins. "Vee thinks you're ridiculous."

There was a rustling noise and then Hawkins appeared in the frame next to my brother's face. "Your brother is the ridiculous one. I learned today that he wants to take his kid shooting cans in the desert when he's like the same age as your kindergarten kids."

"That sounds about right," I said, laughing. "You'll find that's pretty common for Texas boys, Hawk. I'm sure lots of the kids in my class can shoot already."

"Ah, Hawk doesn't get it because he's from California. He may be a Marine but the gun culture in San Diego ain't like in Texas," Travis said.

"Why were you guys talking about kids, anyway? Cat isn't pregnant is she, Trav?" I already knew why they were talking about kids, thanks to Jake telling me all about it the night before, but I couldn't tell them that.

Brooks shook his head. "Nah, not that I know of, anyway. It's our buddy Mills. He's the one with a lil baby devil dog on the way."

Travis turned the phone away from him and Hawkins and pointed it at their other friend. "Hey, Vee."

I waved back. "Hey, Matt. Congratulations!"

"Thank you," he replied.

"Are you excited?"

Matt smiled tightly. "Mm-hmm."

Travis turned the phone back to him and Hawkins. "Mills is a little freaked out to be a daddy, but he'll get there soon enough. Won't you, buddy?"

I heard Matt make some noise of agreement from behind the phone, and I couldn't help but wonder if

Jake was in the room with them, too. I hadn't seen him when Travis had turned the phone around, but that didn't mean he wasn't there. Why didn't he want to come over and say hi like Hawkins had done? I wondered if there was a way I could ask about him without tipping Travis off to the fact that I knew him better than he thought I did.

"So ..." I started. "What are you four doing? Hanging out at the hotel?"

"It's just the three of us right now. Jake's in the shower," Travis replied.

I tried to ignore the flutter in my belly as I thought about Jake being in the shower. Especially because the closer we got emotionally, the more attracted to him I became. I racked my brain for a distraction. "Why are you guys staying in a hotel anyway? Wasn't the last place you stayed a little more ... military-ish?"

Hawk laughed. "What, like a base?"

"Yeah," I confirmed.

"They don't have barracks for us here, so we stay off base in a hotel. Night crew stays on base, though. And I don't envy them," Travis explained.

"Why's that?" I asked.

"They have to stay in these tents on Wolf Pack Park," Travis replied. "Full of spiders and bugs. You'd love it."

I made a grossed-out expression. "Sounds lovely. How much longer are you in Korea?"

I knew the answer to the question because of Jake, but I didn't want Travis to know that.

"We're headed to Hawaii in a couple days. We were supposed to only be there for a week, but we found out this morning we're going early and it'll be two weeks instead."

At this, I perked up. Jake hadn't told me that yet. "Really?"

"Yeah, hey, when's your spring break?" Travis asked. "You should fly out to Hawaii and meet up with us. Tell Mom and Dad to come, too. Cat's already got her flight booked."

Before I could answer, Hawk nodded. "Mills and I already told our wives to come out. You could hang out with them while us guys are all working."

Alarm bells went off in my head as I looked at Hawk's expression. It was almost ... accusatory? I couldn't put my finger on it, but I needed to ask Jake if he'd told him about us.

"My spring break is next week," I said slowly, as if it was the first time I'd considered this plan. "I guess I could check out how much the flights are and let you know."

"Oh, come on, Vee," Hawk said. "It'll be fun."

I remembered Jake telling me about how Hawk and his wife were an integral part of the matchmaking plan to get Mills and his wife back together after they'd split.

The way he looked now, with a subtle gleam in his eye, I wondered if he was up to something now, too. Maybe it wasn't matchmaking, necessarily, but it was definitely something.

"I'm sure Mom and Dad will pay for it," Travis said with a wink.

"Sure," I agreed finally. "I'd love to come out. And I have some savings, I don't need Mom and Dad to pay for it."

Travis shrugged. "Suit yourself. Either way, I bet they'll be stoked. They need a vacation."

"I have something I need to tell you guys," I said, biting my lip.

Nora and Rachel exchanged a glance, then Nora paused the show they were watching on the TV and scooted over on the couch to make room for me between them. She patted the seat. "Sit. Spill."

"It's okay, I'll stay over here. It's safer," I joked. Truthfully, I was too wired up to sit and needed the freedom to pace the room.

"Ooh, this is gonna be good," Rachel said, taking a handful of popcorn from the bowl in her lap and popping it into her mouth.

"Remember when we discovered that Jake—the

Marine from the Connect app—knew Travis?" I asked
them.

Nora's eyes grew wide. "You mean, when we discovered that they were besties?"

"And when you said you weren't going to talk to him
anymore because of the drama it could cause?" Rachel
asked.

I nodded. "Yep."

"Girl." Nora pulled her legs up and crossed them.
"Are you talking to him again?"

"That's not smart, friend," Rachel warned, shaking
her head. "I stand by what I said before, shut it down
before you get too close and it gets messy."

I made a guilty face and fidgeted with my hands.
"I'm not talking to him *again*. I never stopped talking to
him in the first place."

Both of their eyebrows shot into their hairlines at
the exact same time, and they gaped at me, mouths
open.

"Are you serious?" Rachel shout-whispered. "You
told us you stopped talking to him!"

"Oh ... my. So, wait, every time we asked you who
you were talking to ... was it him the whole time? Or are
you still talking to other guys from the app?" Nora asked.

I cringed. "Just him. I haven't been on the app in
weeks."

"Vee ... I don't even know how to handle this right now." Nora brought her hands up to the side of her face. "What about Robby? Were you talking to him?"

"No, sorry guys. I stopped responding to him a few weeks ago," I admitted.

Rachel rolled her eyes. "Not gonna lie, I'm tempted to be mad at you. You lied to us."

"I know." I hung my head and leaned back against the wall in front of them, feeling like I was lined up in front of the firing squad. "I'm sorry."

Nora waved a hand. "*Psh.* It's fine. I get why you lied."

Rachel and I looked at each other and then at her. A little sprig of hope grew inside me. "You do?"

"I do. I'm sure Little Miss Ray of Sunshine over here freaked you out talking about all of the drama it would bring if you talked to him behind Travis's back," Nora answered, gesturing to Rachel with her wine glass as she spoke. "I get why you wouldn't want to admit you were talking to him. I, on the other hand, encouraged you to talk to Jake, remember? He's hot. So, you could have told me."

I chuckled. "Yeah, you did. But I love you guys equally so I wasn't going to tell one of you and not the other."

"While I appreciate that," Rachel said with a smirk,

"I don't think you needed to lie to either one of us about this. We both would have supported you."

I narrowed my eyes and her and laughed when I saw Nora giving her a similar look.

"I think you would have vehemently disapproved of her talking to him," Nora said, using one of her million-dollar words—a force of habit from working with the sixth grade gifted students on their vocabulary.

"I agree," I said, taking a seat in the armchair. "I should have told you guys. I think at first, I didn't plan to keep talking to him. In fact, one time we decided we weren't going to talk anymore, but I had to get off the phone, so we made plans to talk again about not talking … and that turned into deciding to keep talking. But secretly. It's all very silly now that I say it out loud."

Nora wagged her eyebrows. "Sorry, but I think it's all very romantic and swoon-worthy. You're in a secret relationship with the hot Marine who's best friends with your brother. Your brother, who explicitly doesn't want you to date another one of his friends after the hurt it caused both of you last time. I'm here for this."

Rachel rolled her eyes as Nora stole the bowl of popcorn off her lap and started eating it like she was watching my life as a movie before her eyes.

"Is this a relationship, then?" Rachel asked. "You're not just talking, but you're like … secretly boyfriend and girlfriend?"

I shrugged. "We haven't put any labels on it. We text every day. And every morning, while I'm waiting for my kids to come in, we video chat before he goes to bed. We've basically just been getting to know each other ... a lot of flirting, which, ah, I'm addicted to. He's so fun. And then we've had some seriously deep conversations that just totally make me want to squeeze him to death. But we haven't had any conversations about what we are or talked openly about how we feel about each other."

"And how *do* you feel about him?" Nora asked, still eating her popcorn and living for this conversation.

Sighing, I dragged my fingers through my long hair. "I don't know. I mean, I seriously feel like I'm living my life just looking forward to the next time I get to talk to him. My phone makes a sound and my stomach just ... flips. But I've never even met him in real life. What if it's not that great in person? What if it's weird?"

"How long until you can find out? When do they get home from deployment?" Nora asked.

I covered my face with my hands, then peeked out at my friends through my fingers. "Actually, they're on their way to the Marine Corps base in Hawaii, and I'm flying there for spring break."

Rachel's mouth popped open. "You're going to see him in Hawaii? Are you nuts?"

"No, I'm going to see Travis," I said quickly. "He was

the one who invited me. My parents and Cat are going to be there, too. Getting to see Jake is just a perk that none of them know about."

Nora drained the rest of her wine. "Oh, yes. This is going to be good."

"Why are you telling us now?" Rachel asked, hugging her knees to her chest.

I shrugged. "I'm telling you because, well, I'm sorry for lying to you, and I couldn't take it anymore."

Rachel's lips formed a hard line on her pretty face, and she picked at the edges of the throw pillow next to her. I had a feeling I wasn't done making amends for this with her.

"Are you planning to come out as a couple in Hawaii?" Nora asked.

"No," I said firmly. "I don't even know if we are one. Besides, we shouldn't be, right? It would hurt Travis."

Rachel raised her brows, saying a lot without saying anything at all.

"Well, I think you need to talk to Jake about that," Nora said. "You guys need to figure out if you're a couple, and if you are, are you going to stay a secret forever?"

I sighed. "You guys need to help me figure out what to do when I see him. Before I can even talk to him about all of this, I need to know how I'm supposed to act with him. Do you think he thinks we're a couple?

Should I act like we are? Should I be casual like we're just friends and let him make the first move? Help!"

Nora put the bowl aside and wiped her hands. "Lemme see some of your conversations so I can get the vibe of how you guys talk. Come here, show us the goods."

I smiled and pulled out my phone, but didn't move from my seat yet. "Rach, are you mad at me?"

My friend tilted her head and considered me. "No, I'm not. I'm disappointed. And I still think you might be opening yourself up to some drama you'll regret later."

I hung my head.

"But," she continued, "like I said before, I support you. So ... Nora's right. We need to see some conversations. Come here."

I grinned and bounced over to the couch and sat between them, opening my messaging app and preparing to dish on weeks of my secret texting situation with Jake. I looked up at them. "Thanks, guys. I've been missing your advice through all of this."

Rachel nudged me with her shoulder. "We used to have to hold your hand through every message when you were talking to guys on Connect. I have a feeling this thing with Jake is pretty real if you haven't needed us to tell you what to say."

My chest warmed. She was right. I'd been able to be myself with Jake. And it felt really good.

Three days later, when our plane touched down at Daniel K. Inouye International Airport, my stomach was in absolute knots. I tucked my hair behind my ears, fiddled with the ends, wondered if I should have gotten it trimmed before I came, and then scowled at my left thumb where my fresh manicure had already started chipping.

"You ready?" Mom asked, making me jump.

I looked up to find that it was our turn to disembark, so I grabbed my backpack and followed my parents off the plane. We were greeted by Hawaiian Airlines employees with a traditional flower lei greeting. A smiling woman placed the exquisite purple-and-white plumeria around my neck and I breathed in the fragrant floral aroma. I could get used to this. I looked at my mom and grinned. I imagined the lei greeting was an optional add-on package to our flight since not everyone was getting them, and I knew my mother was to blame. She was extra like that.

I linked arms with my mom as we stood off to the side of the baggage carousel. "*Mahalo* for the lei greeting, Mama. I'm so ready for paradise."

"You can thank your dad for that," my mom answered, winking at me. "He's the one who booked it."

"No way. I can't believe it," I said, looking at my dad

as he grabbed a bag from the belt and added it to our pile. "This trip is good for his soul if he's booking stuff like that. I would've thought he'd call that a waste of money."

"Oh, he called it a waste of money, all right. He's still the same man. But we haven't taken a vacation together in years, so he said he wanted to make it special."

I smiled at my mom. Her perfectly styled, shoulder-length brown hair had streaks of gray throughout it, almost as if they were strategically placed. For all I knew, maybe they were. She was the kind of beautiful Texan housewife who always looked effortlessly put together. I was sure she was the cause for my attention to detail in my own appearance, since she'd first taught me how to do my hair and makeup when I wasn't even ten years old. For that reason, I'd never been a tomboy. Girly all the way through, and even now I loved wearing sundresses more than any other article of clothing.

Speaking of my clothes, I looked down at my leggings and tank top. I couldn't wait to get to our hotel and freshen up after the long ten-hour travel day from Texas. There was no way I wanted to see Jake for the first time in real life looking like I'd spent all day on a plane.

Travis had booked us a room at the hotel on base. I'd stayed at the Marine Corps Lodge on the base in San Diego before, but he said the base hotel rooms on

Kaneohe Bay were more like bungalows on a private beach. Jake or no Jake, I couldn't be more excited for my first trip to Hawaii.

"Ready, ladies?" Dad asked as my mom and I took our suitcases from the cluster of rollers he pushed towards us.

"Ready," we replied.

"Cat's already at the base, right dear?" My mom asked my dad.

He checked his watch. "Yes, she got in a few hours ago and took an Uber to the base."

"He didn't pick her up?" I asked.

"No, this is still his deployment, sweetie," Mom answered as we walked up to the rideshare section of the arrivals curb. "We'll see him when we can, but we need to think of this as our vacation that he'll crash now and again."

I shrugged. Fine by me. I had a suitcase full of books and bikinis, and I was ready for a vacation. Oh, and maybe a hot Marine who I was secretly falling for, too.

10

JAKE

Brooks put his phone back in his pocket and dropped his head onto the back of his desk chair. "Well, my wife just met up with my family at the MCX. Cat is probably draining our bank account as we speak."

I chuckled. The Marine Corps Exchange was pretty much the equivalent of Target but tax-free and carries name brands at lower prices. "Nah, man. Cat's coming from San Diego. There are a million exchange stores there, why would she go crazy here?"

"Oh, several reasons," he said, counting them out on his fingers. "One, she's on vacation mode. Two, she's with my mother, who can't go shopping for groceries without coming home with something extra. And three, because she's with my sister, who isn't bad with money or anything ... she's just another girl to shop with. And when girls shop in packs, it's nothing but trouble."

My stomach tightened at the reminder that Ivy was only a quarter of a mile away from me instead of six thousand. What would it be like to see her in person? When I'd gotten out of the shower the other day and Brooks had told me his sister was going to come out to see him, I'd almost had a heart attack. He'd gone on and on about how we'd all hang out, go to dinner, see the island. Would I be able to hang out with her around Brooks without giving us away? I had no idea. The thought of seeing her in real life, right in front of me, made my hands twitch in anticipation of getting to touch her.

I glanced around our shop, feeling the urge to get away from him. "Hey, man. I'm gonna go out and ask Hawk and Mills when they'll be done with their last few jets. I'm ready to get out of here for the day."

"Fine by me," he replied. "The sooner we get out of here, the sooner I get to kiss my wife."

I nodded and left the room, my nerves completely shot.

The ocean breeze hit me as soon as I entered the open-air hangar. I crossed the catwalk and braced my hands on the railing that overlooked the jets below, staring out toward the ocean. It was hands down the nicest view from any hangar I'd ever seen. There was something incredibly calming about the ocean. That is, a view of it from land. I hadn't thought of it as calming when I'd spent months on end aboard an aircraft carrier.

"Murphy," a voice said from behind me, making me jump.

I turned. "Afternoon, Staff Sergeant."

"I hear you're getting out," Staff Sergeant Cooper said, leaning against the railing. "Is that for real?"

"Yes, Staff Sergeant." I braced myself for some kind of lecture from my superior, who'd lately turned into a huge mentor for me. He was a great Marine, the kind who always got the big awards and outstanding fitness reports. He was a Marine's Marine, if you will.

He made a face like he smelled something foul. "Why?"

It wasn't an odd reaction. I'd gotten it from pretty much everyone I'd talked to about getting out of the Marines after eight years in service. Usually, if you weren't going to make a career out of it, you got out at the end of four years. After eight years, many people liked to call that halfway to retirement, even though it wasn't, since retirement was at twenty years. But hey, who's counting?

"Got a DOD job out in Fort Worth," I replied.

Cooper stood up from the rail. "No kidding?"

"No kidding." I felt my chest swell with pride. It was

a great career move, I'd be making better money, and it wasn't common to get the opportunity to do it.

"Well, all right, then. That's a good reason, Murph. I came up here to try to change your mind."

I chuckled. "Yeah, I'm looking forward to it. Plus, I'd heard I was about to get put on the list for recruiting or drill instructor duty."

Cooper, who'd gone through recruiting duty not too long ago, let out a boisterous laugh. "Man, run for the hills. DOD versus recruiting duty? *Psh.* Do not look back. Do not pass go, do not collect two hundred dollars."

"That bad, huh?"

"Yeah, recruiting is that bad," Cooper leaned back against the rail again and crossed his arms over his chest. "I mean, in all seriousness, if it weren't for the DOD job, I would still try to convince you to stay in. You're almost halfway to retirement. But this is a good move, and I'm happy for you. Do you know anyone in Fort Worth?"

"Yeah," I answered without thinking. I glanced at the door to my shop where Brooks still sat. "Well, no. Not really. My buddy is from there, so he's going to hook me up with some people."

"Good. And at least it'll be similar to what you're used to on active duty. Except you'll actually get to settle down for once. Twelve years in the same place ... I can't even imagine it. I'm already wondering where I'm gonna go next and if my girl is going to want to go with me."

"Oh, yeah, how's that going?" I asked, remembering that I'd met his girlfriend over the holidays when he'd needed help after a Toys for Tots fundraiser.

He smiled widely. "Great. She seems to be handling the deployment pretty well. It's weird, though, because I never thought I'd want a girlfriend on deployment again. I got cheated on last time."

"Ugh, that sucks. I'm sorry man."

Cooper waved a hand. "It's fine. Hazard of the job, right?"

"I hope not."

"You have a girl?"

I scratched my head. "I don't know, maybe. It's early. And ... complicated."

"What relationship isn't? How does she feel about you moving to Fort Worth? She's in San Diego, right?"

I glanced at the door to the shop again to make sure it was still safely closed, separating Brooks from this sketchy conversation. We were headed into dangerous waters. I didn't want to start making up lies to cover myself, just in case I couldn't keep them straight.

Finally, I decided to be honest yet vague. "Actually, Brooks—the one who's from Fort Worth—suggested I look for girls out there since that's where I'm moving. So, she already lives there."

Cooper patted my arm. "Nice. Hope it goes well. And gets ... uncomplicated."

"Thanks. And I hope things go well with your girl, too."

"Thanks. I'm thinking about proposing at the homecoming. Is that too cheesy?"

I shrugged. "You wouldn't be the first or the last."

Cooper rolled his eyes and held out his hand for me to shake. "Good answer. All right, Murph. Congrats again on the DOD job. And the girl."

I shook his hand and forced a smile as he walked away. It might not have been the best move to tell Cooper there was a girl. At the rate these Marines gossiped, it was only a matter of time before one of my friends started asking questions.

I turned to head downstairs and see about leaving, when I smacked right into Brooks's huge form.

"What girl?"

11

IVY

"I'll call him," I said to my mom as we dropped our shopping bags on the hotel bed. "I'm sure he'll want to meet us."

My dad shook his head, taking a seat next to Cat on the sofa and turning on the TV. "Between you and Cat, I don't know how many times I have to explain to you girls that he's on deployment. He's not going to be free to join us whenever you want."

Cat laughed and nudged my dad, telling him to lighten up.

I made an obstinate face at my dad and hit Send on the call to my brother.

"Hey," I said when Travis answered the call. "What are you up to?"

"I'm getting ready to leave work," he replied. "What are you guys doing?"

"We just got done shopping and wanted to grab a bite to eat. Wanna come?" I stuck my tongue out at my dad and he rolled his eyes.

"Absolutely," Travis said. "I'm starving. Hang on— hey, Jake, you wanna come to dinner with my family? You should meet them since you're moving there."

I inhaled sharply, then recovered when my dad and Cat looked at me questioningly. I cleared my throat and played it off. "Oh, you're with Jake?"

"Yeah," Travis replied. "We're walking out of the hangar now. He said he'll come. There's a restaurant on base, I'll text you guys the info, and we'll meet you there after we go grab a quick shower."

"Sounds good," I said, my voice a little strained. "See you in a bit."

"Seems like he *is* free to join us whenever he wants, Pops," Cat teased her father-in-law, then turned back to me. "Where are we meeting?"

"He said he'll text it to me, they're gonna go shower. He's bringing a friend," I explained, feeling like my throat was full of sand. I made a beeline for my suitcase and gathered up my toiletry bag, a sundress, and my blow-dryer. "I'm going to go freshen up."

"Is it a fancy place?" Cat asked, looking down at her tank top and shorts. "Should I change?"

"No, I mean, I don't know. You're probably fine." I backed up toward the bathroom, my knees hitting the bed behind me and making me jump and go around it. "I just brought a lot of cute dresses and I want to make sure I get to wear them all."

Cat raised a brow at me. "Okay. Sheesh, you'd think you were the one excited to see your man after months apart."

I chuckled, but the sound came out shaky with nerves. "Yeah, ha, no. Not me."

Before I could embarrass myself any further, I ducked into the bathroom and closed the door behind me. Leaning my head back against it, clutching the bundle of clothes and toiletries to my chest, I shut my eyes. For a moment, I simply stood there, breathing deeply through my nose to calm myself. It was time. I was going to finally meet Jake. For dinner. At a restaurant. With my brother.

My phone buzzed in my hand, and I looked down at it, fumbling with everything else in my arms.

Jake: I can't wait to see you.

Thanks to the extra time I'd taken to do my hair and makeup for this dinner that was likely doomed to end in disaster, the guys were already at the restaurant when we arrived. Cat had gotten to see Travis earlier in the day on his lunch break, so I'd missed their big reunion. Still, it was cute to see him light up at the sight of her walking toward him as he stood—alone— under the green awning outside the restaurant.

My mind raced with the possibility that Jake had decided not to join us for dinner. Maybe he got cold feet. Maybe he regretted talking to me behind his best friend's back and didn't want to meet me after all. I wanted so badly to be able to ask Travis where he was, but I knew it would probably raise some red flags. The last thing I wanted was for Travis to wonder if I was into his best friend. I looked at my parents and silently willed them to ask him about Jake.

"Didn't you say you had a friend coming?" Cat asked.

Best sister-in-law ever.

"He's in line to get us a table," Travis replied, hooking his thumb behind him. "It's pretty packed in there and there's not a lot of room, so I figured we'd just hang out until he called us."

That was it. I couldn't take it anymore. I'd been on the same tiny island as this guy for almost five hours now. I wasn't going to wait any longer to see if what we had was as amazing in real life as it was online.

"I have to pee," I announced. "I'll be right back."

Without another word, I marched toward the

restaurant and pulled open the heavy glass door. The cool air-conditioning sent a shiver down my spine as it blasted me in the face. There were at least twenty people crowded together in the small lobby of the restaurant. Apparently, we weren't the only ones visiting Marines on their deployment. Groups of families stood together in cramped circles as they waited for their tables. I craned my neck and searched their faces, looking for a familiar pair of piercingly blue eyes.

A warm hand snaked out from behind a waiting family and tugged me into the hallway where the restrooms were. Breathless, I looked up to find the eyes I'd been searching for. He didn't say anything at first, just looked at me. His small smile was almost one of disbelief as his gaze raked over my face and down my body, then back up again to meet my eyes.

I laughed and took a step back to take him in, our hands still joined. He was taller than I'd expected, and I loved how he was dressed. He'd paired his dark jeans and flip flops with a charcoal Aloha shirt that had black palm trees scattered all over it. To complete the look, he'd tucked black Ray Bans into the breast pocket. He looked like the poster boy for how to make touristy Hawaiian shirts look smoking hot.

Despite my instant attraction to real-life Jake, I was also surprised by how at home I felt in his presence. "Hey, Jake."

"Hey, Ivy," he said, and I enjoyed how clear and warm his voice sounded when it wasn't coming from the speakers of my phone.

He stepped closer and reached out, slowly, with the hand that wasn't still holding mine. Our eyes stayed locked together until his fingertips made contact with my cheek. The fire that ignited forced me to close my eyes and lean into his palm.

"I can't believe you're really here," he whispered, moving closer still.

I opened my eyes again, eager to look at him after getting to know him so well with just our words on the screen between us. I had expected our first meeting to be awkward. I'd thought about it the entire flight over here. I pictured us shuffling our feet and trying to act cool, but every scenario I'd imagined had involved us finally seeing each other face-to-face with my brother or someone else around. This scenario we were in now ... alone, blissfully close, and three-dimensional, had never crossed my mind.

His other hand left mine and came up to the opposite side of my face, and he lowered his forehead to mine. "This is not good."

"Nope." I giggled, not pulling away, but reveling in his nearness.

"Brooks," a voice from behind us called, forcing us

to spring apart. "Brooks, party of six. Your table is ready."

He rubbed the back of his neck and let out a shaky breath. "I'll go tell them."

"Okay, I'm gonna go that way," I said, nodding behind me toward the bathroom.

"I'll meet you at the table."

I nodded. "See you there."

He backed out of the hallway, his eyes not leaving mine until he had to turn the corner toward the door. I released a ragged breath I hadn't realized I was holding. Jake was right. This was not good.

12

JAKE

Ivy: This is too much.

I controlled my face as I read the text, my phone concealed in my lap. The seating arrangements at dinner were out of control. It was a table for six, with three on each side. I sat across from Brooks, who sat next to his wife, with his mom choosing the seat next to Cat. Brooks's dad sat across from his wife, leaving the only empty seat for Ivy when she came back from the bathroom right in the middle of me and her dad.

Me: Not how I pictured our first dinner date.

Ivy: Oh, is this a date?

Me: Weirdest. Date. Ever.

Ivy: Ugh this better not be your idea of a date, Jake Murphy. #notimpressed

I resisted the urge to chuckle at Ivy's words and instead turned it into a reaction to whatever story Brooks was telling his family. I didn't know what he was talking about, but it was something about our time in Japan. Brooks loved to tell stories, and he was great at it with his Southern accent and humor. Everyone was fully enthralled in his story, leaving my texting with Ivy to go perfectly unnoticed.

Me: It's not. I promise.

Ivy: Then what is your idea of a date?

Me: Now that you're here, I'd have to say something super cheesy and romantic like dinner on the beach.

Ivy: We'd probably end up eating sand.

Me: Oh, fine then. That's what I get for being romantic. I pictured some pretty great kisses on the beach at sunset and all that.

Ivy stole a glance at me, her face nothing short of a sarcastic warning. I pursed my lips and looked away, focusing on the bright yellow walls of the restaurant to keep from busting up laughing. It was a lot harder to secretly flirt via text when you were sitting right next to the person—and their family.

Ivy: You better slow your roll, buddy. We haven't even had a first kiss yet and you're already daydreaming about making out on the beach at sunset?

Me: About that first kiss ...

Out of the corner of my eye, I saw Ivy shift in her seat. She attempted to focus in on the conversation going on around her, answering something her father said, taking another bite of the chips and ceviche appetizer we'd been working on, and then gave it another minute to torture me most likely, before she went back to her phone.

Ivy: What about it?

Me: Do you think there's a way we can sneak away soon? Because I almost kissed you in the hallway. I want another chance.

Ivy put her phone under her leg and brought her hands up on the table, again, focusing in on the conversation and the food. After a few minutes of not reaching for her phone again, I took the hint that the conversation was over. Had I struck a nerve? She was the one who brought up a first kiss. And she'd even said we hadn't had it yet.

I picked my phone back up to say something— what, I wasn't sure—when Brooks kicked me under the table.

"Murph," he said, a wide smile on his face as he leaned in. "We never got to finish our conversation."

I gulped. "What conversation?"

"The one where I heard Staff Sergeant Cooper say

something about you having a girl. Are you texting her right now?" Brooks wagged his eyebrows at me and nodded toward my lap.

Busted. "I was checking the score. We're losing."

"Ah, man. That blows," Brooks said, taking a huge bite of his burger.

Relief settled deep in my chest as I realized he wasn't going to press the issue. Hawk would have, for sure. He was nosy like that. But Brooks was much less interested in other people's personal lives.

I thought I was in the clear, but then Cat zeroed in on me. "What girl?"

"There's not really anyone in particular," I replied with a shrug, noticing Ivy's back go up a little. "I think you just didn't hear him right, Brooks."

"So, Jake," Rick piped up, leaning forward to look at me around Ivy. "Travis says you're moving to Fort Worth. You got a job at the JRB?"

"Yes, sir," I replied. Everyone in Fort Worth knew of the Joint Reserve Base. It was the source of the sizable military community in the city.

"That's a smart move, son," Rick said, toasting me with his beer. "Any way you can get yourself a pension and good retirement plan is the way to go. It's good you're thinking about it now and not getting out without a plan. I wasn't military, I was in oil, but I still know a thing or two about working your way up the food chain and setting yourself up for life."

I smiled. "Thank you, sir."

It was hard to focus on Ivy's dad while she sat between us, looking gorgeous in her bright, floral sundress. Even if I'd never talked to her before that day, I still would have thought she was attractive enough to be distracting. But the fact that I'd spent every day of the last couple of months either talking to her or looking forward to talking to her made the whole thing more intense.

"We'll have to have you over for dinner when you get to town," Rick continued, winking at his wife. "Judy's a great cook."

"When do you move to Fort Worth, Jake?" Judy asked.

"Sometime this summer," I replied. "I have a few things to square away with my unit in San Diego before I get out, and then I'll be there."

Ivy's lips twitched and she covered it by taking a sip of her drink. I noticed she'd been quiet throughout this conversation with her parents. Maybe it was her guilty conscience keeping her quiet. If we weren't trying to hide the fact that we'd been talking behind everyone's back, I wondered if she'd offer to show me around town. Would Ivy volunteer to be my tour guide if she was getting her first impression of me today? Or would she be as disinterested as she seemed?

"I told Jake he could count on my folks to give him a good welcome," Brooks said to his parents before turning to me. "Anything you need, man, I mean it."

"Thank you all. I appreciate it," I said, guilt pouring over me. What was I doing?

After dinner, we'd gone our separate ways, and I was restless. I needed to see Ivy. We needed to talk about what we were doing and if we should keep doing it. I looked around my empty hotel room. Brooks and Cat had gone to see a movie at the theatre on base, so I knew he was occupied for a couple hours. I wondered what Ivy and her parents were up to and if she'd be able to sneak away for a while.

Sitting on my bed, I pulled my phone out and sent her a text. I thought back to when I first spotted her entering the restaurant alone. I'd been leaning against the wall, waiting for our name to be called. The bell over the door had chimed, and I'd expected to see Brooks coming in with his family. Instead, it had just been her.

I'd known her immediately. I'd spent so many nights staring at her features through a phone screen, I felt like I had them burned into my mind. Her long brown hair hung in loose curls over her shoulders, and her deep brown eyes scanned the crowded room, looking for something. My heartbeat picked up speed. Was she looking for me? Had she come in alone to find me?

Quickly, I scanned the lobby of the restaurant for a place we could talk. My eyes zeroed in on the hallway leading to the bathrooms, but before I made my move, I'd waited another beat to see if Brooks was going to come through the door behind her. When he didn't, and she'd kept searching, I moved from the wall and grabbed her hand.

Those brief, stolen moments in the hallway had been nothing short of exhilarating. I hadn't known what it would be like to hold her in my arms ... but I'd needed to find out. And once I had her there, I didn't want to let go. I'd gotten so close to kissing her before the moment had been broken by the hostess calling for our group.

I checked my phone to see if she'd replied or even started typing out a response to my text. When she hadn't, I laid back on the bed and closed my eyes. I wondered if it was a good thing that we hadn't gotten a chance to kiss. I already felt kind of addicted to her. Talking to her was the highlight of my day. It would only get worse if I had the memory of her lips on mine to torture me with. And with Brooks promising that he and his family would be able to help me with anything I needed once I moved to Fort Worth, the level of sliminess to this whole thing made me feel worse and worse.

My phone buzzed and I jolted upright.

Ivy: Meet me here.

I opened the attachment with a pin dropped from the phone's map program. It was a spot on one of the beaches near her hotel. She and her family were staying at one of the larger, nicer hotels on Marine Corps Base Hawaii. Brooks and I were at the one that more closely resembled a campground with the rest of the guys we were on deployment with.

Without giving it a second thought, I replied that I'd start walking over and headed for the door. It took me about fifteen minutes to walk from my hotel to the spot she'd indicated on the map. I spent pretty much the entire time overanalyzing, stressing, telling myself to stop stressing, and then stressing some more. But when I finally arrived and saw her standing on the beach, her hair blowing in the coastal wind and a big smile on her face, all of that negativity vanished.

"Hi," she said, giving me a shy wave and tucking a strand of hair behind her ear to keep it from blowing into her face.

"Hey," I replied.

"Why am I nervous?" she asked, her eyes holding a smile but her lips pursed in confusion.

I shrugged. "Would it help if I said I was, too?"

"Yes."

"Then I am."

She drew circles in the sand with her bare feet. "I was never nervous when I was texting you."

"Hmm." I pulled out my phone, opened up the messaging app, and sent her a text.

Me: Better?

I watched as she read the message, rolling her eyes and shaking her head at me.

"Listen, we should actually talk about all of this," I said, reaching out and tracing a line from her shoulder down to her hand, then taking it in mine. "Wanna take a walk?"

She nodded. "Let's."

We took off down the shore, flip-flops in one hand, the other joined between us. For a few minutes we walked through the wet sand, water lapping up over our feet. I breathed in the salty air and took in the sense of peace I felt with her. It was the picture-perfect stroll along the beach. The only thing missing was the sunset to make the perfect backdrop, but we'd missed it by a few minutes, unfortunately.

"So, talk," she said, nudging me playfully.

I looked out toward the ocean and then back at her. "I really like you."

She blushed. "I really like you, too."

"But ..."

"Travis," she said, sighing heavily.

"Right."

"Do you want to break it off?" Her eyes searched my face, and I saw genuine sadness in them over the idea. That told me everything I needed to know about how she felt about me.

I squeezed her hand. "No. Definitely not. But I think we need to come clean."

She wrinkled her nose. "I was afraid you'd say that."

"Ivy," I said, pulling her to a stop and turning her to face me. "I know we've just been doing this whole secret, long-distance thing, and it's only been a couple of months. But I feel like this could really be something when I move to Fort Worth. And I don't want it to be a secret."

She blew out a breath, not convinced.

"I want to be able to take you out to dinner—without your parents," I continued with a grin. "And go to the movies or rodeos or whatever you Texas people do for fun."

Ivy let out a laugh and kicked at a wave, spraying me with water. "Rodeos?"

"Hey, what? I bet you look great in shorts and

cowboy boots," I said, enjoying the way I was able to watch her face when I joked around with her for once, instead of staring at my phone screen. "I'd go to a rodeo to see that."

Ivy covered her forehead with her hand. "You're killing me."

"For real, though," I said, digging my toes into the sand. "I think we could have a lot of fun out in the open."

She looked up at me and bit her lip. I brought my hand to her cheek and traced her mouth with my thumb, dying to kiss her.

"I'm not sure about this," she admitted. "I don't think he'll be okay with it."

"It's either we tell him and then see where this goes, or we see where it goes and he finds out later anyway. I feel like he'll be less likely to punch me the earlier I tell him."

She chuckled, leaning her cheek into my hand. "You seem so sure it'll work out between us."

I took my hand away from her face. "Hey, I mean, if you don't think it's worth finding out ..."

"Stop," she hit me in the leg with her sandals. "It is worth it, for sure."

"I have an idea."

"What's that?"

I put my hand around her waist and pulled her

toward me. "Let's not decide anything until we have that first kiss. Then, I bet, we'll know."

She tipped her head up and smiled. "Fine. If it's a terrible first kiss, at least we can walk away without Travis ever finding out about our almost-relationship."

I smirked at that, not even bothering to dignify that with a response. There was no way it would be a terrible first kiss. Not that I was some kind of kissing professional or anything, but the heat between us told me our first kiss would be nothing short of amazing. And enough was enough. I'd been wanting to kiss her for way too long, and I wasn't going to let any more time pass before it happened.

Her long hair whipped in the wind, brushing against my arm as I held her close. I leaned down until our lips were so close, we were breathing the same salty air. I meant to lightly brush my lips against hers to test the waters, but once I made contact with the silky smooth texture of her full lips, I couldn't hold back.

Whatever I'd thought I'd feel in that moment was nothing compared to the fierceness of the emotions coursing through me as my lips moved over hers. I felt her hand come up around my back, pulling me in, closing the barely-there distance between us.

She kissed me back with a force that matched mine. We were eager for more, and yet, somehow, we still took it slow, both of us drinking in the sensation of finally getting to express what we've felt for the last two months.

The roar of the dark ocean faded into white noise, the perfect background music for this kiss. Like the waves, it was deep and powerful ... and just as if I were out there, floating in its vast openness, alone, I knew my feelings for Ivy could just as easily consume me.

13

IVY

A larger wave than the ones that had been lapping over our feet splashed up and smacked me in the back of the legs, making me gasp and break what was surely the best kiss I'd had in my entire life. Yes, I realized that was saying something, considering a year ago I'd hoped to be getting engaged soon. But now, standing on this beach in this man's arms, I was really glad I hadn't.

Jake's embrace steadied me as I stumbled in the sand, my feet having been swallowed up a bit after standing still while we were kissing. I brushed at the water on the back of my thighs and looked up at him, the beautiful blue color of his eyes still visible, even in the twilight.

"Well," I said, exhaling sharply and tossing a glare

over my shoulder. "Thanks for ruining the moment, ocean."

"Nothing is ruined." He chuckled and grabbed my hand, pulling me against him.

I kissed him briefly once, twice, and then a third time because I couldn't get enough. Before I got all caught up and dizzy again, I pulled back and pressed my cheek to his chest. He held me tightly with his chin on the top of my head, staring out at the ocean behind me. For a moment, we just stayed that way, holding each other. Breathing in and out and listening to the waves.

"So," I said, staying cuddled up to him, enjoying the rhythmic *bump-bump* of his heartbeat, "who's going to tell Travis?"

He made a humming sound. "Rock Paper Scissors?"

I pushed away from him with a laugh, kicking some water.

"Oh, no you don't!" He dodged the spray and lunged for me, catching me around the waist and spinning me around.

I tied to wriggle out of his grasp, but my efforts sent us tipping backwards. Jake tried to recover, overcorrected, and then cushioned our fall with his back as we hit the sand with a thud.

"Ugh," he groaned, grimacing even as he suppressed a smile.

I scrambled up just in time for the tail end of a wave to crash over him, and he came up sputtering as I held my sides from laughing so hard it hurt.

"That," he choked out, shaking sand and water from his hair like a wet dog, "did not go how I planned."

"I think it went great," I replied with a raised chin, "considering it could have been me who got clobbered by that wave."

"Ah well, good, I'm glad you got away," he said. Bending over and putting his hands on his knees, snorting loudly. "I have sand in my nose."

"Karma."

He moved like he was going to make a grab for me again and I dodged him, kicking off what would be another twenty minutes of running through the water, falling down, and kissing in the surf. It was completely like that opening scene in Grease when Danny and Sandy were at the beach, except that the light was quickly fading around us, making it harder to see.

When we were sufficiently soaked and worn out, we sat peacefully together in the dark, watching the waves roll in. The glow from some nearby buildings and the full moon gave us just enough light to be able to stay out there and relax without being completely shrouded in darkness. I sat back against his chest, his arms wrapped loosely around me.

"Well, you got your beach kiss. Was it everything you hoped it would be?" I asked.

"And more," he replied, his lips pressing against my temple.

"And have you given any more thought to who should tell Travis about us?"

Jake sighed dramatically. "Actually, I've been avoiding thinking about your brother."

"Well, time to start," I pressed. "You're the one who said it would be a good idea to come clean."

He paused for a moment. "Do you think we shouldn't?"

I wasn't sure how to answer that. When he'd first brought it up, my initial reaction was a hard no. There was no way I wanted my brother to know I was falling for another one of his best friends. We might have been kids the last time it happened, but he hadn't handled it well then and he likely wouldn't handle it well now, either. In fact, he would probably handle it even worse since the other relationship imploded, taking his friendship down with it.

"I'm not sure. I really don't think it'll go well, Jake. And I'm not ready for what that will do to us."

I felt his body tense against my back. "I mean, we know what our two options are, right? Stay together and tell him or stay together and don't."

"I like that staying together is in both of those options."

He laced his fingers with mine and held me tighter, speaking quietly, his lips against my ear. "I have no idea how to go back to a life without you in it."

I breathed in deeply and let his words wash over me. The last couple of months talking to Jake had been amazing. I'd felt alive and wanted and special for the first time since before Cory left me. And the idea of Jake not wanting to go back to a life without me in it just reminded me that Cory had left to go find one. I shivered, my wet dress sticking to my skin.

"You cold?" he asked, rubbing his hands down my arms.

"A little."

"We can go ...."

I shook my head. "No, not yet. I'm not ready to go back to reality."

He tightened his hold on me and leaned forward, resting his chin on my shoulder. I felt ... completely at ease. Like I was meant to be there with him. Looking back, I'd known I didn't need him to heal my broken heart enough for me to love again. My friends had done that. Months of retail therapy, cooking sessions, movie nights, and good, old-fashioned crying on their shoulders had put me back together enough for this new relationship to take root. I felt like I was in the perfect

place to start something new with Jake. We just needed
to deal with my brother.

"Okay," I said, taking a shaky breath, "so I think the
biggest issue with the Cory situation was that Cory left
me and then left town without even bothering to tell
Travis. That really hurt him."

"Makes sense," Jake said.

"If he would have explained himself to Travis," I
continued, "if he'd told him their friendship mattered to
him and he didn't want things to change between them,
maybe things would be different right now. Maybe
they'd still be friends even though Cory and I are over,
and then Travis wouldn't care if I dated another one of
his friends. All of that leads me to think it should be
you who tells Travis."

Jake cleared his throat. "Okay."

I turned in his arms so I could see his face. "Okay?"

"I wanted to be the one to tell him anyway."

"You did?"

He chuckled. "I'm not afraid of your brother. I knew
it should be me who tells him. Our friendship does
matter to me, and I don't want things to change between
us. I just wanted to make sure you and I were on the
same page about telling him, that's all."

I settled back against his chest. "Oh. Okay."

"I do have one request, though."

"What's that?"

"Can I wait until after you and your family leave Hawaii?"

I shifted to look at him again. "Why?"

He leaned in and kissed me softly. "Because if it does ruin everything, I want a few more nights like this with you before that happens. Think we can try to keep it a secret until then?"

I kissed him firmly on the mouth. "Like I tell my students—do or do not. There is no try."

Jake groaned and threw his head back. "A *Star Wars* reference? Seriously? I think I'm falling for you, teach."

"I'm good with that," I replied, kissing him again.

14

JAKE

"It's freaking humid today," Brooks said, peeling off his shirt and tossing it in the general direction of his open laundry bag.

"You missing that icy air in Japan?" I asked, scrolling through my phone to read sports updates. We'd just gotten back from a half-day of work—what they called "Aloha Fridays."

Brooks thought for a moment, then shook his head. "Nah. I still prefer the heat. You'll see—I go home more often in the summer than in the winter. Most people steer clear of hundred degree heat, but not me."

I balked. "Ugh, that sounds terrible."

"You'll get used to it after a couple years," he said, waving his hand. "I still can't believe you're moving to my old stomping grounds. We'll have to go out and tear it up when I visit. And maybe you'll have a serious thing going with one of those Connect girls and we can double."

My lips formed a thin line and I nodded. "Mm-hmm."

"What are you doing tonight, by the way?" He dug though one of the drawers of the dresser we shared and pulled out some clean underwear and jeans, tossing them on his bed.

"Nothing." I controlled my face, trying not to let on that I was hoping he'd invite me to do something with him and his family.

That was how it had been all week. Every day, we went to work as usual, then when we got back to the room, he got ready to go out with them and I hung around hoping for an invitation to join them. Daily, I considered simply asking what they were up to and if I could tag along, but I chickened out every time. I didn't want to give him a reason to question why I wanted to. Thankfully for me, Brooks had that Southern hospitality thing going on and always extended the invite.

Over the course of the week, we'd gone out to dinner as a party of six every night. I was really starting to get comfortable with his family, and Ivy and I had pretty much perfected the art of flirting via text while everyone else thought we were barely interacting at all.

One night, we'd gone bowling at the alley on base,

and Brooks had paired us all up. He apologized for sticking me with his sister, who was notoriously bad at bowling. It had gone okay, we'd acted casual enough and didn't flirt at all, but he did give me a *don't you dare* look once when I'd accidentally checked her out as she bent down to get a ball. But that wasn't an indicator of a secret relationship, just that I was a normal dude.

Last night, we'd played a round of golf with his dad at the base's veteran-only Kaneohe Klipper Golf Course. It was a championship course with insanely high ratings from veteran golf pros, but I wasn't one of them. I'd worked so hard to play it cool in front of the two men that I'd shot like absolute crap, a fact they promised to never let me live down.

"Well, since it's their last night in town, my mom wants to do some fancy luau at the Disney resort. It's pretty pricey, but if you want to come, you're more than welcome. I already invited Mills and Hawk. They went to the Exchange to buy Aloha shirts, and then they'll meet us here."

I pretended to think about it, even though the answer was going to be yes no matter what the plan would have been. I wasn't going to pass up my last chance to see Ivy until the deployment homecoming a few months later.

"Sounds good," I finally replied. "I haven't spent much this deployment, so I think I can swing it."

"Word," he replied. "I'm gonna hit the shower."

I settled back against my pillow and pulled up my texts.

Me: Disney luau tonight, huh? You must be stoked.

Ivy: Completely. I need a pic with Minnie in her hula skirt.

Me: Will you be wearing a hula skirt?

I stifled a laugh when she sent me back an animated GIF image of a fat guy in a grass skirt doing the hula.

Before I could reply, a knock sounded at the door.

"Hey, guys," I said, opening the door wide for Hawk and Mills to enter. They were each dressed in jeans and brightly colored Hawaiian shirts, fresh from the Exchange.

"Murph." Hawk nodded and patted me on the shoulder as he passed by, then took a seat on the bed, making himself at home.

I closed the door behind Mills and then knocked on the bathroom door. "Brooks, they're here."

"I'll be right out," he called, and I heard the metal clang of the shower curtain hooks sliding along the bar as he closed it.

I took a seat next to Hawk and pulled out my phone, checking for any texts from Ivy. As I turned the screen around, one popped up.

"'Texas'?" Hawk asked, grabbing my phone.

"Man, give me that." Panic flooded my senses as I snatched it back from him. "Mind your own business."

Hawk held out his hands and raised his eyebrows at Mills.

"Touchy much?" Mills asked. "Who's 'Texas'?"

I pumped the air down with my palm and looked nervously at the bathroom door. "Keep your voices down."

Mills and Hawk shared a suspicious look and glanced at the door, then back at each other, and finally their gazes fell on me. Understanding appeared to wash over them both at the same time and their eyes bulged.

"No," Mills said at the same time that Hawk covered his mouth with one hand, his eyes alight with the scandalousness of the situation.

"Oh, you are so busted," Hawk said, his palm muffling his voice.

"You didn't shut it down?" Mills asked in a hushed voice. "Murphy, what did we tell you?"

I threw myself back on the bed and stared up at the ceiling, almost relieved for it to be out in the open. "I know, I know."

Hawk hit me on the knee. "Well, I'm proud of you, Murph."

"Are you serious?" Mills lamented. "He's an idiot."

"You're an idiot," Hawk retorted. "You would do the same thing and you know it. Shoot, so would I."

I sat up. "You know, come to think of it, Brooks would, too."

Mills and Hawk considered this for a moment, then both nodded in agreement.

"I think the big question is, are you going to tell Brooks?" Mills asked.

"Tell me what?" Steam poured out of the open bathroom door as Brooks came out with one white hotel towel wrapped around his waist and another draped over his shoulders.

I cleared my throat. "That, I ..."

"He doesn't have a shirt for the luau," Hawk finished, rolling his eyes dramatically like I'd really stepped in it this time.

"Wear that gray one with the black palm trees," he said.

"It's dirty," I replied, playing along with Hawk's story.

Brooks shrugged. "It's cool, man. Just wear whatever."

"See, that's what I told him," Hawk explained, "but he wanted to look as cool as we do."

Mills, who had his back to Brooks, stared at me as if this whole thing was way too ridiculous for him. I held his stare, trying to convey a message of *shut up or I'll deck you.*

"All right, it's fine, keep your boots on," Brooks said,

pulling out one of his standard Texan-isms. "We can stop at the Exchange on our way off base and grab you one."

"Thanks, man," I said, eyeing my friends. I wondered if it was a good thing they knew, so I had them to talk to, or a bad thing because they'd ruin it? Only time would tell.

15

IVY

"Aloha." Three beautiful women greeted us as we stepped toward the courtyard where the luau was held. Traditional leis dangled around their forearms from wrist to elbow, and they draped one over each of our heads before directing us down a stone path through the tropical landscape.

As we came into the clearing, I gazed around the Halawai Lawn at the Disney Aulani Resort. In typical Disney fashion, it was immaculate and picture-perfect. I'd read somewhere that this resort tried to put Hawaiian culture first and Mickey Mouse second, so it was nice to see the magic of Disney come alive in subtle ways throughout the resort.

There was no way I'd be able to stay there on a young teacher's salary, but I hoped maybe someday I'd have enough in savings to make it possible to come back and do a whole vacation there. Maybe when I had kids. Maybe if I happened to be married to a hot former-Marine who moved to Fort Worth and our incomes were combined ... I shook my head. *Too far, Ivy.*

The eight of us approached a long table with bright orange-and-red drinks in short plastic cups. I picked one up, then handed one to my mom beside me. "Cheers."

"Ooh, these are so pretty. What's in this?" she asked the bartender behind the table.

"This is our signature drink of the event. Pog and passionfruit rum, ma'am," he replied with a wide smile.

"What's 'pog'?" my dad asked as our group meandered away from the table, sipping his drink and making a satisfied noise as he tasted the sweet flavors.

"It stands for Passion Orange Guava, Mr. Brooks," Hawk supplied, halfway finished with his drink already. "It's a huge thing here. I buy the stuff at the commissary by the twelve pack."

"It's full of sugar, though," Mills added.

Travis snickered, patting his buddy on the shoulder. "You're the only one who's new to the fitness obsession, Mills. The rest of us have been doing this for a while. We can handle a sugary drink here and there."

I noticed Jake trailing behind us, sipping his drink

and people-watching. I wanted nothing more than to walk up next to him, take his hand, and enjoy this time as a couple. My brother and his wife looked like they were on some kind of family-friendly honeymoon and my parents were gushing about taking trips together more often. I was practically green with envy.

We reached the center of the lawn where all of the tables were arranged. My parents had entered a drawing earlier in the week and had won VIP seating for our group without an up-charge, so we located the table with our name on it right in front of the stage.

Just as every dinner that week, the seats were chosen and somehow Jake and I wound up sitting next to each other. We gave each other casual smiles and sat down, but when I looked up and met Hawk's eyes, he made a face that left no doubt in my mind that he knew about me and Jake.

I pulled my phone out and discreetly sent a text to Jake.

Me: You told Hawk?

Jake: Mills knows, too.

Me: Oh, really? Practicing for telling Travis?

Jake: Long story.

Me: Are they cool with it?

Jake: Hawk is. Mills thinks I'm an idiot.

Me: Think we can sneak away?

Jake: Yeah.

I slipped my phone back into my crossbody purse and stood from the table. "I'm going to use the restroom."

My mom looked around. "Oh, honey, you'll probably have to go back to the lobby through those doors."

"Okay," I said, following her gaze. "How long until the show starts? I don't want to miss it."

My dad checked his watch. "Ten minutes until the pre-show stuff. You'll be fine."

"Unless you have to take a—" Brooks started to pull some typical big brother grossness, but his quick-thinking wife elbowed him in the gut before he could finish.

"Thanks, Cat," I said, rolling my eyes. "I'll be back."

I didn't know what Jake would tell them in order to get away from the table, but I hoped it would be believable, whatever it was. And I hoped Hawk and Mills would cover for him, rather than out him, if necessary. I walked through the crowd of tables and out the way we'd come, pulling open the heavy doors to the opulent lobby.

Cool air rushed over me as I entered the expansive space. Its high-arching ceiling was reminiscent of a traditional Hawaiian canoe house, the angled walls providing a warm and welcoming vibe. I gazed at the artwork etched into the walls, upbeat Hawaiian music pouring over me, completely immersing me in the spirit of aloha, Disney style.

I strolled toward a large, open-air patio that overlooked the beautiful landscape of the resort. The music followed me, filling my cup with the satisfaction of a relaxing getaway. It had been an amazing week. I wasn't ready for it to end, but I knew I would go back to my students completely refreshed and revitalized.

Hands came around my waist, familiar and solid, and I leaned back against his chest. For a moment we just stayed that way, taking in our surroundings and enjoying the feel of each other. He kissed my cheek then turned me to face him.

"Thank you for coming to see me," Jake said, sliding a strand of hair behind my ear.

I smiled up at him. "I'd make a joke and say I came for the Hawaiian vacation, but I'd be lying."

"Does that mean you would have visited me in Korea, too?"

"I would love to visit Korea. I recently fell in love with K-Dramas on Netflix." I said.

"I'm not going to pretend I know what a 'K-Drama' is," he replied.

I grinned. "Seriously, though, I'm glad I came. This has been a dream."

He leaned in and kissed me softly. I lost myself in the feel of his lips on mine, the enchanting music in the background, and the warm tropical breeze against my skin. Through my haze, I heard the sound of beating drums and a conch shell signaling that the luau was about to begin.

"That was the fastest ten minutes of my life," he said, leaning his forehead against mine.

"Maybe it's a five-minute warning." I didn't want this time with him to end. The instant we went back to the luau we'd have to pretend to be casual acquaintances again.

He gave me one last squeeze. "Come on, we can head back together. We've been hanging out all week. We were even bowling partners. It's not that weird to be seen together."

I narrowed my eyes at him. "You think we've been going overboard with how much we're not talking in front of them?"

"I think we spend so much time texting under the table that we forget how little we're actually saying to each other out loud. Hawk said he thought it was weird."

"He did?"

Jake nodded. "Yeah, he told me we're selling it a little too hard. If there was nothing going on between us, we'd at least talk. Right now, it looks like we barely notice each other."

"Oops," I said, grinning. "What can I say? I've never had a secret boyfriend before."

As soon as I'd said the words, I wished I could shove them back into my mouth. I hadn't meant to refer to him as my boyfriend until we'd had some kind of conversation about it. That was one thing I'd learned from living with Rachel and Nora and watching them navigate their own dating adventures. You never wanted to assume a guy thought of himself as your boyfriend. Because if he didn't, well, the risk of that embarrassing conversation wasn't worth using the title.

The corner of his mouth twitched. "Boyfriend, huh?"

"Did I say boyfriend?"

"You did."

"Well, fingers crossed you want that because otherwise this is going to get real awkward real fast."

"Come here," Jake chuckled and pulled me in for another kiss. "Of course I want that. Let's just make sure my talk with your brother goes well tomorrow before anything's official. I'd like him to be on board, you know? For the sake of my own guilty conscience."

"You got it," I replied, hearing another round of drum beats and pulling him by the hand toward the doors we came in through. "Come on, let's hurry up and get back to the table before we miss Moana."

"Who's that?" he asked, letting go of my hand and

stuffing his hands in his pockets as soon as we got within range of the luau festivities.

I rolled my eyes. "Be prepared to find out when you move to Texas. We're going to have all kinds of Disney movie nights. And K-Dramas, too."

"Oh, boy. Can't wait," Jake said, pumping his fist with a sarcastic expression.

I stuck my tongue out at him as we approached the table, catching Travis's eye as I took my seat.

"Did you fall in?" he asked, paying no attention to the fact that Jake and I had come back to the table together.

I glared at my older brother. "Shut up."

Another round of drums sounded and everyone turned their attention to the beautifully decorated stage at the front of the lawn. Dancers joined the drummers on the stage, and a lovely introduction to the luau began. After some chanting and a short welcome song, the narrator of the show announced that the buffet was open, and we were dismissed by tables. As we made our way to the lavish spread of food, I couldn't help but stare out at the sunset over the ocean. What a perfect way to end my vacation in paradise.

"Move it or lose it," Brooks said, nudging me forward in the buffet line.

I rolled my eyes. "You sure know how to ruin a moment."

"You were having a moment with yourself?" he asked, poking me in the back with the plate he'd picked up from the edge of the food table.

"Ha-ha," I replied over my shoulder.

Travis leaned down to whisper in my ear, "You have something you need to tell me?"

Alarm bells went off in my mind, and I didn't turn to face him so he wouldn't see the guilt all over my face. I reached for a set of serving tongs and placed a helping of Kalua Pig and Maui Onions on my plate. "Not sure what you mean. Want some?"

He took the tongs from me and served up his own dish, then handed them to Cat behind him. "You've been glued to your phone all week."

I shrugged. "Uh, okay. So what?"

"So," he said, taking the spoon from me to scoop some island-style macaroni salad onto his plate, "who have you been texting? Have you been talking to Cory?"

I bristled and finally looked up to meet his eyes. "Cory?"

"I'm not at all cool with you two getting back together," he said, then nodded his head above me. "Move up, sis."

I blinked and kept moving through the line, the subject completely threw me off my game. I scooped some white rice and steamed vegetables onto my plate then handed him the spoon, afraid to even ask what he was talking about. After a moment, curiosity got the better of me.

"What would make you think I was getting back together with Cory?" I asked, realizing that Jake was on the other side of Cat in the buffet line. I wondered if he could hear this conversation.

Travis shrugged. "I don't want to get in the middle of it or anything ...."

"Get in the middle of what?" I put a dinner roll on my plate, the last item on the table, and moved to the side, tapping my toe as I waited for him to finish filling his plate and walk back to the table with me.

"He posted a photo of his new place in Fort Worth," Travis said, rolling his shoulders like the whole thing really ticked him off. "Aren't you still friends with him?"

"No. I didn't want to see all the posts about his life in New York." My throat felt tight as I said the words. "He's back?"

"Guess so. I figured it was him you were talking to. Now that he's gonna be in town again, are you gonna get back together with him?" Travis asked, just as Jake walked up behind us from the buffet line.

His steps faltered as he looked between us, but he didn't say anything. He just swallowed, his jaw clenching, and sat down at the table.

"Babe," Cat interrupted from her seat, waving him over. "Come here, you have to try this fish."

"We'll talk about this later," my brother said as he left to sit with his wife.

I took my seat next to Jake, trying to catch his eye, but he wouldn't look at me. I considered pulling my phone out and trying to text him under the table, but Travis was apparently paying more attention to my texting habits than I'd thought, and I didn't want him to notice that Jake was texting, too.

A shirtless man with tribal tattoos covering his chest blew a conch shell from the stage. The din of the crowd quieted down and the stragglers from the buffet line hustled to take their seats. I wanted to focus on the stunning celebration of Hawaiian culture unfolding in front of me, the sun setting in the background, and the aroma of the food filling my nose.

But instead, all I felt was dread. My week in paradise was ending, and there was something in my gut that told me my secret relationship was in danger of ending, too.

16

JAKE

"I mean, can you believe that tool?" Brooks asked no one in particular. He ducked his head under the bench press bar and sat up, grabbing a towel at his feet and wiping the sweat off his brow. "Who does he think he is? Moving back to town without even letting me know. It's all just as sneaky as when he left."

I made eye contact with Hawk, who'd been spotting Brooks as he lifted. I did one more pull-up, gritting my teeth as I struggled to make my chin come above the bar, then dropped to my feet. "He didn't call you?"

Brooks shrugged. "He called. I didn't answer. He could have texted me, though."

I guzzled some water from my stainless steel bottle, wincing from the icy temperature as it made its way into my chest. Brooks had stuck to Ivy like glue last night after the luau, so we hadn't had a chance to talk about the conversation I'd overheard between them. The only communication I'd gotten from her about the whole thing was a text that said she'd video call me when she got home so she could explain. Checking my watch, I calculated that she would still be on her flight for at least another three hours.

"When was the last time you even talked to the guy?" Hawk asked, watching me over Brooks's head.

"Man, don't judge me, but I haven't answered a call from him in almost a year now. Granted, he stopped trying to hit me up after a while. I don't know .... Do you think I'm being too hard on the guy?" Brooks asked me.

I shrugged. It wasn't an easy question to answer from my position, so I tried to figure out how I'd respond if I were just an outside observer of the whole thing. "I mean, you got mad at him in the first place because he left your sister and moved to New York without giving you a heads-up, right?"

He leaned back under the bar to do another set, his voice straining from the weights as he answered. "In a nutshell, yeah."

"Okay, and you're mad now because he moved back to town 'without giving you a heads-up,' even though he's tried to call and you never answered?"

"Yeah, pretty much," Brooks grunted under the

weight he was lifting, Hawk stood at the ready in case he needed to catch the bar before it hit him in the chest.

"If you haven't talked to the guy in a year, why do you care if he moves back to Fort Worth?" Hawk asked.

"Because," Brooks said, letting Hawk help him ease the bar back onto the cradle, "I care if the reason he's moving back there is so he can try to patch things up with my sister."

Something like rage stirred deep in my gut. If that punk thought he could move home after a year and Ivy would jump right back into his arms, he was dead wrong. When all you can do is text and talk on the phone with someone, you got to know them on a level a lot deeper than you otherwise might. She didn't want Cory anymore. She was over him. I liked to think that I was part of the reason for that, but I knew from talking to her that she had made a lot of progress in that area before we'd even met.

"Do you think she'd go for that?" I asked, trying to act casual. As far as Brooks knew, the only interactions I'd ever had with Ivy was what he'd seen that week. I couldn't let on that I knew her any better than Hawk or Mills did.

"Man, that's what worries me," he replied, stretching one of his huge arms across his chest. "She just might."

Hawk gave me a warning look. I must not have been

keeping my composure as well as I needed to. I rolled my neck and took another sip of water to cool down before I spoke. "What makes you say that?"

"Look, Ivy has been in love with Cory since we were kids, man. That doesn't go away because the guy makes one mistake."

I scoffed. "It was a pretty big mistake."

Brooks nodded. "Oh, absolutely. I agree. I'm not ready to forgive him for taking off on her—on both of us—without a thought to how we'd feel about it. But all I'm saying is, if he pulls some big, grand, romantic crap ... she just might."

Fury whipped through me like a hot wind, and before I had the sense to restrain myself, I tossed my water bottle on the ground and strode out of the gym, letting the heavy door slam shut behind me. The ocean breeze felt good on my damp skin, and I breathed it in through my nose.

Yesterday, I'd planned to talk to Brooks about the fact that I was falling for his sister. I'd planned for it to be kind of a rough morning, depending on his reaction. What I hadn't planned on, was my best friend basically telling me his sister was about to choose another guy over me. And from a tiny island in the middle of the Pacific, there was absolutely nothing I could to stop it.

17

IVY

T he first thing I did when I got home was text Jake and tell him I'd video chat him after my shower. I felt like crap, and if I had to tell my (hopefully) new boyfriend that there was nothing to worry about with my back-in-town ex-boyfriend, I needed to freshen up first.

Twenty minutes later and feeling much less like a zombie, I pushed the video call button on Jake's contact page. It rang for a long while, and I checked the time. He probably needed to get away from Travis. Finally, his face appeared on the screen and my whole body warmed.

"Hey," he said, a small smile playing at the edges of his lips. "How was your flight?"

"Long," I replied. "I'm sorry we haven't gotten a chance to talk after last night."

The melodic tone of our doorbell chimed, and I frowned, listening to see if one of my roomies would answer it.

"What is it?" Jake asked.

"Someone's at the door."

"Are you expecting anyone?"

I shook my head. "It's probably for Nora or Rachel."

"Ivy," Nora said, knocking on my door. "Someone's at the door for you."

I made a face at Jake. "Sorry, it's for me. Can I call you right back?"

"Yeah, sure." He looked frustrated, and I couldn't blame him. Travis bringing up Cory's return to town right in front of him probably hadn't been easy.

"I'll be five minutes, tops." I blew him a kiss before ending the call, then hopped off my bed. I was eager to deal with whatever had interrupted us and call him back.

When I opened the front door, Nora and Rachel were on the other side of it, blocking my view of whomever was standing on our front porch. They moved aside when they heard me come out, giving me a full look at my uninvited visitor.

Standing before us, holding the most gorgeous

bouquet of flowers I'd ever seen, was Cory. And if I'd had any doubt about whether he was in town for good, the Fort Worth Fire Department logo on his shirt would have been my answer. In fact, it appeared he was already back to work given that he was wearing his turnout pants and suspenders over the gray shirt, complete with a baseball hat with the department's logo on it. Seeing him standing at my front door was like stepping into a time warp.

My stomach flipped as our eyes met. Yes, I'd moved on. Yes, I could have safely said if I'd never laid eyes on this man again, I'd be fine. But when his dark-brown eyes met mine, some deep-seated part of me melted.

Cory gave me a small wave with the hand that wasn't holding the flowers. I looked at my friends. They stood stock-still, staring at Cory with matching expressions of disdain.

"Can we talk?" he asked, his voice thick with emotion.

Nora curled her lip at the bouquet. "Shouldn't you be fighting restaurant fires in Hell's Kitchen right about now?"

"Nah, I was in Midtown, actually," Cory said conversationally, ignoring her attitude. "Had a few buddies over in Hell's Kitchen, though. Nice guys. But they ate out too much."

Nora harrumphed and zeroed in on me. "Are you okay?"

"Yeah, thank you," I responded, finally finding my feet and walking past my friends out onto the porch. "I'll be right in."

With one last glare at Cory, my sweet protectors granted us our privacy and closed the door with a snap.

I looked up at him, the floral scent from the bouquet overwhelmed me as it filled the space between us. He moved to hug me, but my hesitation mixed with his unease made it an awkward clashing of shoulders and arms.

"What are you doing here?" I asked, when the painfully weird hug was over.

Cory tilted his head toward the street, and I followed his gaze. I balked. How had I not noticed when I'd first come onto the porch? "Oh, my ... Cory, seriously?"

The huge ladder truck belonging to his firehouse was parked on the street with five firefighters lined up in front of it, each with an identical bouquet to the one he held in their arms. I stared at them, feeling a mix of pain and regret, but also happiness to see the guys who had at one time been my second family.

My neighborhood was very walkable, and a group of girls passed by us and made swooning noises. The sight of this admittedly handsome firefighter and all of his friends bringing such beautiful flowers to his girl was probably like something out of a movie. It should have made me want to curl up and die from cuteness overload, but instead it made me want to kill him.

"Look. I want a chance to explain. No pressure." He held out the bouquet, which I still hadn't taken from him.

I looked at the pretty mix of colors and shapes in the arrangement. My traitorous eyes welled up with tears, and I used all of my inner strength to make them go away before I looked at him again. "This feels like a lot of pressure, actually."

He swept the flowers behind his back. "Look, they're gone. Don't even worry about the flowers."

I glared at him.

"Fellas," he turned to them and gestured with a slice of his hand along his neck. "Ditch the flowers."

I chuckled despite myself as the guys made a show of stuffing the bouquets into one of the storage compartments on the side of the truck, then slamming it shut and looking around as if to say, "Flowers, what flowers? Nothing to see here."

I looked up at my ex. "This is a little much, Cory."

He shrugged, gazing over at the big rig and then back down to meet my eyes. "I dunno, I thought a big gesture would be the way to go."

"Mm-hmm."

"Plus, I thought you'd be excited to see the guys."

"I am excited to see the guys," I said purely for their benefit. They may have been on the other side of the lawn but it was still within earshot. "I just don't understand the purpose of all this."

"The purpose, Vee? Isn't it obvious? I'm back."

I blinked at him, my face holding no expression. "And?"

Cory dropped his head back and sighed. "All right, come say hi to the guys. They miss you. Then I'll tell them to take off, and we can talk when we're alone."

With a resigned sigh over being ambushed, I followed him across the front yard to say hi to his fire family. I pulled out my phone on the way and sent a quick text to Jake.

Me: Gonna need more than five minutes to handle this, sorry. I'll explain later.

I stuck my phone in my back pocket and found a smile for Cory's brothers from the station. "Hey, guys."

By the end of the fifth bear hug, my mood was much lighter. Despite my annoyance with Cory, I spent the next ten minutes joking around with the guys like old times.

Tyler, one of the paramedics, had been a "probie" when I'd last seen him. I congratulated him on his new status. I'd been there on his first day and through most of his probationary period. It hit me right in my teacher's heart to see that he'd succeeded. And Bobby, another firefighter I'd known for years, had been promoted to lieutenant. He'd been passed over a few times thanks to politics and some stuff out of his control, so I was genuinely happy for him. We caught up and laughed and for the briefest time I forgot all about how mad I was about them ambushing me. It was just good to see them.

With one last honk and wave, the truck disappeared around the corner, leaving me alone on the porch with mixed emotions and my freaking ex-boyfriend. I glanced over at him. He still looked fantastic in the darn turnout pants and suspenders, and I hated myself for thinking so. But really, I wouldn't be human if I didn't.

Frustrated with the whole thing and wishing I could go inside and call Jake, I plopped onto to the cozy porch swing my friends and I had installed a few months back. I pulled a decorative pillow onto my lap like a shield, then realized doing so made room on the swing for him to sit, so I tucked my legs up next to me.

Cory gingerly took a seat in one of the mint Adirondack chairs under the window, patting the arms of the wooden chair. "I like the new porch setup."

I looked around our quaint porch. We'd spent a week out here perfecting it, starting with tearing down the old railings and installing new ones. Then we'd sanded and painted the whole thing, including the door. The demo had been good for my soul. At the time, I distinctly remember picturing Cory's face on the railing each time I brought the mallet down. The swing, café table, rug, and chairs had all been purchased one payday at a time ever since.

"Thanks," I said, deciding not to tell him the part about the mallet.

"Did you have fun in Hawaii?"

I smirked, my mind instantly flashing back to my blissful nights at the beach with Jake. Playing in the water, kissing, and gazing up at the stars. I had never seen a more beautiful night sky in my entire life. I wondered bitterly if Cory would like to hear all about that part of my vacation.

"It was fine," I replied. "Wait, how did you know?"

"You posted pics .... Sorry, I know we're not friends on there anymore, but I still checked in here and there. Sounds creepy when I say it out loud, though."

My lips formed a hard line, no idea what to say.

"It looked relaxing, anyway. I'm jealous."

I squirmed in my seat, ready to get this over with. "Why did you come back, Cory?"

"Do I have to spell it out?"

I rolled my eyes.

"Okay," he said. "I came back because I made a mistake. I never should have left Fort Worth. I never should have left you. We had a good thing going here, and I messed it up."

"In other words, you thought the grass was greener in New York, but it smelled like sewer instead of manure?"

He chuckled. "I really missed you, Vee."

"Did you seriously think you could come over here with flowers and your guys and I'd take you back? After a year of silence, you show up and expect it to be water under the bridge?" I tried hard to keep my tone conversational, but I could feel the resentment radiating through my fingertips.

"I don't know what I thought," he admitted, his familiar Southern drawl sounding hollow.

"You must not think very highly of me if you think that would work."

He frowned. "Of course I think highly of you, Vee."

"You have a funny way of showing it." I tightened the grip on the pillow against my chest, using it to hold myself together.

Cory sighed. "New York wasn't what I thought it would be. It was great, don't get me wrong. I got a lot of experience fighting fires. Saw more action in a year than I probably will in a decade here. But I just ... didn't feel ..."

"Happy," I finished for him.

"Yeah, guess not."

I tilted my head toward the street. "A big gesture with flowers and all that wasn't the right move. You're back here with your tail between your legs, and there aren't enough flowers in the state to hide that."

He winced, but didn't say anything. I considered him for a moment. I had no idea why, but a huge part of me felt sorry for him. I'd pictured this moment many times over the last year. Not that he'd return and want me back, but just if I ever saw him again, what it would be like.

I imagined I'd yell at him. I imagined I'd say hurtful things, so he knew how much his leaving had hurt me. But now, as I headed down that road, I found myself quickly losing steam. He needed to understand that we were over, but I didn't need to go out of my way to cause him pain.

"Cory, we've been like family our whole lives. You, me ... and Travis. Some part of me will probably always love you. But as far as being a couple—that ship has sailed." I fidgeted with the tassels on the throw pillow in my lap.

His brown eyes stared deep into mine, almost like

they were searching for a sign I was lying. "You mean that?"

I nodded.

"Is there someone else?"

I raised a brow. "It doesn't matter."

"It sure does matter," he said, his tone icy. "It matters to me."

Throwing out my hands, I let out an exasperated huff. "I'm not talking about this with you. It's a messy situation, and it's your fault it's messy."

"My fault? How could it be my fault?"

And just like that, my steam picked up again. "You were Travis's best friend, Cory, you moron. You left both of us when you went to New York. And you didn't even tell him. Our freaking mom had to be the one to let him know what was going on. How do you think that made him feel?"

Cory yanked off his baseball hat, ran a hand through his chestnut-colored hair, then wedged it back on. "I have a lot of fixin' to do with Travis, I know that. I should've told him what I was up to. I never should've left in the first place, I know that too, but still. The man hasn't taken any of my calls since before I went to New York. And what on God's green earth does that have to do with your new boyfriend?"

I sighed. "I can't talk to you about it, Cory. I shouldn't have said anything. The point is, you hurt me and my brother when you left. And neither one of us is going to forgive and forget that easily."

A heavy silence blanketed us as we sat there for a long while. I used the time to take stock of my emotions. It had gotten a little heated for a minute there, but all in all, my heart rate was slowing back to normal and my breathing was more even.

I watched him, sitting in the chair across from me, thinking hard about everything we'd said. He was handsome, sure. But the sight of him didn't light me up inside like when I was with Jake. In fact, if there was one thing my week in Hawaii had taught me, it was that my feelings for Jake were bigger and stronger than anything I'd ever felt for Cory. And that's how I knew I wasn't simply over Cory—we were never right for each other in the first place.

"Vee," Cory said, leaning forward in his chair, resting his elbows on his knees, "I messed up. I own that. But I'm not some pathetic loser who's going to pine after you if you've moved on. If you tell me you don't love me anymore and you don't want to be with me, I'll let you go."

My answer didn't even need considering. I gave him a small smile. "I'll always love you, Cory. We grew up together. But I'm not in love with you."

"All right." He swallowed and looked away. "Part of me thinks I should fight for you or something ..."

"It wouldn't work," I said, laughing. "If I thought it would, I'd let you know. I promise."

Cory took his hat off again and picked at the edges of the bill. "Can I tell you something?"

"Why stop now?"

The corner of his lips twitched up. "Ha. Listen ... this might sound weird, but this didn't really go like I planned."

"Clearly ...."

"I thought I'd go down swinging. I made this whole plan with the guys and the flowers and the truck. I told myself there was nothing I wouldn't do or promise or say if it meant I could get you back."

I pursed my lips. "I see."

"And yet, here we are, just ... not getting back together. And it's fine. It shouldn't be, considering what I expected to happen here today, but it is. I'm sorry, I feel weird admitting that."

I brought my legs down from the swing and patted the seat next to me. "Come here, Cor."

He returned his hat to his head, backwards this time, and sat next to me on the swing. He put his arm around me and I laid my head on his shoulder. For a moment, we sat there in silence, swinging back and forth, staring out at the yard.

"I think the way you feel makes sense," I said finally.

"How's that?"

"If we were meant to be, you wouldn't have been able to leave me that easily. And Cory, you didn't even look back when you left for New York."

He squeezed my shoulder, but didn't reply.

I cleared my throat. "And it took a long time for me to admit this to myself, but we weren't in a great place when you left."

"It looked picture-perfect from the outside, though, didn't it?"

"It did," I agreed. "But you were right about what you said before you left. We stayed together because we were both too scared to break up. If you hadn't done what you did, who knows where we'd be. We might've gotten married just because, and then ended up divorced later."

"Yeah, maybe so."

"Why did you really come back? Because I don't think it was for me, deep down."

He didn't answer right away, so I waited patiently.

"This is home," he finally said. "I didn't want to put down roots someplace else when I already had them here. I guess I thought being with you was part of that."

I patted his leg. "Well, in a way, it is. You're Travis's best friend. That means we'll always be family. You need to fix things with him, and then we can have our new normal. As friends."

"Sounds good to me," he replied. "And since we're

friends ... can you drive me back to the station? You made me ditch my ride."

I snorted. "Sure. And then I'll help you spruce up the firehouse with all those flowers you wasted your money on."

18

JAKE

I answered the video call as soon as it rang since I'd already been scrolling my social media feed. Ivy's face appeared, and my chest tightened at the sight of her. I'd been stressed ever since we'd said our very brief goodbye after the luau last night. Thoughts about her and her ex had been creeping around my mind all day. I wished I could rewind time and go back to our first night on the beach. That way I could relive the whole week with her, just in case it was all I'd ever get.

"Hi, I'm so sorry that took so long," Ivy said, her expression sincere. Then her brow furrowed. "Wait, did you talk to Travis this morning? Did you tell him?"

I breathed out through my nose, remembering my crappy morning at the gym with her brother. "Nope."

Her eyes narrowed. "No?"

"The conversation got a little sidetracked."

"I see ...." Ivy bit her lip and looked down.

"Who was at the door?" I felt like I already knew the answer to that question, but I needed to hear her say it.

"It was Cory," she said.

Her expression wasn't the least bit guilty. She didn't look like she pitied or felt sorry for me. She didn't look like she was about to break things off with me so she could be with him. I allowed myself to relax a little bit and hoped that meant good things for me.

"How'd that go?" I asked.

"It actually went well. I promise, you have nothing to worry about with me and Cory. We had a nice talk. Got some things off our chests."

She looked genuine, and I wanted to believe her more than anything. "Good."

"Full disclosure—he did show up here with flowers trying to get me back."

I swallowed down the anger that threatened to make its way out. "Did he?"

"He did." She tucked a strand of her long brown hair behind her ear, and rested her chin on her hand. "With a bunch of his friends from the fire station. It was kind of an attempt at a grand gesture, or whatever."

"Uh-huh." I rolled my shoulders, remembering what Brooks had said about Cory showing up with some big romantic gesture and Ivy being likely to fall for it.

She held up a hand. "But by the end of it, we were sitting there talking about how we both knew we weren't meant to be and things weren't that great before he left."

"They weren't?"

Ivy shook her head. "If they were, he wouldn't have left, you know?"

I did know. Because there was no way I could see myself leaving this girl. "True. So ... he knows it's over between you guys?"

"Yep. And he was good with it."

Relief mixed with the unease in my gut. I couldn't help but still be worried. Cory was there, in person, while I was stuck on an island thousands of miles away. What if he was only pretending to be good with it? What if he was biding his time, planning to make a move when she let her guard down?

Ivy bit her lip. "Are we okay?"

"I want us to be okay," I admitted. "I guess I'm just ... nervous. I'm not there, Ivy. He is. I feel powerless in this whole thing."

"Jake, this past week with you in Hawaii was unbelievable. I'm sorry it ended on such a bad note. I'm sorry we're even talking about this right now. Please, trust me. You don't have to feel powerless. Seeing Cory again after finally getting to be with you in real life was like ... ugh, I don't know. There's no comparison."

I breathed through all of the mixed emotions swirling inside me, figuring it was time I said something I'd been holding back all week. "I love you, Ivy."

Her mouth popped open in surprise, and for a moment my heart squeezed, thinking I'd made a mistake. Then her eyes welled up and she looked at the ceiling, trying not to cry.

"*Gah*, of course!" She fanned her face with her hand. "Of course you wait to tell me that until I can't jump on you and kiss you. I waited for this moment every night on that freaking beach, Jake Murphy."

I laughed, my limbs tingling from the urge to reach through the phone for her. "I know, I know. I almost said it so many times."

She blew out a breath and placed her hand against her cheek, and I wished more than anything that I could hold her face in my hands. I thought back to the way she'd leaned her cheek into my palm and closed her eyes the first time we met, standing in the hallway of the restaurant. It had been on the tip of my tongue even then, but my insecurities over falling too hard too fast had kept me from saying the words.

"I love you, too," she said finally.

After a few seconds of just looking at each other with awkward, cheesy grins, I scratched my head.

"Well, I mean, we started this whole thing on the phone. Might as well have this conversation on the phone, too."

Ivy chuckled. "I guess so."

"So, uh, now I really need to talk to your brother."

"Yeah, I guess you do. Good luck."

I raised an eyebrow at her. "He's not going to punch me, is he?"

"Uh," she said, wrinkling her nose, "I hope not."

"Murph," Brooks greeted me with a nod of his head. "Where you been?"

I slipped the hotel key back in my wallet, then tossed it on the dresser. "Went for a walk."

"Mills and Hawkins are on their way," he said. "We figured we'd spend our last night in Hawaii over on Waikiki. See what kind of trouble we can get into. Wanna come?"

I smirked. "Oh, I don't know … you three married saps are gonna be pretty hard to handle."

"Ha-ha," he deadpanned. His phone buzzed in his pocket and he fished it out, then scowled. "You've gotta be kidding me."

"Everything okay?" I asked.

He turned the phone around so I could see the

picture on the screen. "My buddy back home sent me this."

I leaned in, my brows shooting up as I registered what it was. Ivy stood on the front lawn of what I assumed was her house. A firefighter in turnout pants and a baseball cap held out a bouquet of flowers to her, several of his buddies lined up in front of a fire truck, also holding bouquets. Just as Ivy had warned me, it was quite the romantic gesture.

"Hmph," I said, sitting down on my bed, working to control my features. "Who sent you that?"

"One of the guys he brought with him," Brooks explained. "We've all been friends a while. He said, and I quote, 'You're missing all the fun here.' Can you believe that?"

"Did he tell you how it went?"

"I can only imagine how it went. Man, I could kill that SOB," Brooks said, looking at the photo again. "Who does he think he is? Showing up after a year with all this nonsense. I told you, didn't I? I called it."

I nodded. "Yep, you called it."

"He didn't even give me a heads-up he was in town," Brooks said, tossing the phone down.

"Well," I said, holding up a finger, "he did call you. You didn't answer."

"Oh, man, please. It was too little, too late. I can't believe he's trying to get my sister back before he even patches things up with me. His best freaking friend. He's a real piece of work. When I get home, I'm gonna go straight to that firehouse and give him a piece of my mind. He doesn't deserve to be with my sister. And he ain't gonna be pretty enough for her anymore, either, once I'm done rearranging his face."

I chuckled. "Take it easy, *Country Thunder*. You don't have to do that."

Brooks shot me a warning look. "Whose side are you on, anyway?"

It was now or never. "Ivy's."

"What?"

I leaned forward, resting my elbows on my knees as I faced him. "I'm on Ivy's side, man."

He scoffed. "You barely know her."

I didn't reply, just looked at him.

"You barely know her. You just met her this week." Brooks had been leaning back against the headboard, his feet on the bed. After I remained silent once more, he swung his feet down to the floor and sat across from me, eyes boring into mine. "What are you not telling me?"

I took a deep breath. "Remember when you had me change my Connect settings to Fort Worth?"

Brooks stared at me, blinking slowly. "So help me, Murphy. If you're about to tell me you've been talking to my sister on a dating app since January, I'm going to rip your freaking head off."

I sat up straight, not looking forward to what would happen if he decided to make good on that. Before I could speak, however, a knock sounded at the door. Neither one of us moved. We just sat there, staring at each other. Me, wondering if he was about to lunge across the short distance between us and decapitate me as promised. And him, well, I didn't know what he was thinking. But I really hoped it wasn't going to end with my face rearranged instead of Cory's.

"Hello," Mills called from the other side of our hotel room door. "Anybody home?"

Another round of knocks hit the door, and my eyes shifted behind him, silently asking if I should get it or leave it.

Brooks waved a hand. "Saved by the bell."

I got up and opened the door, holding it wide for our friends to enter. "Hey, guys."

"What's up?" Hawk asked, then he read my face and the tightly wound posture of Brooks, who'd begun pacing in front of the window like a hungry, caged tiger. "Oh, uh-oh."

Mills raised a brow, also taking in the vibe in the room. "What's going on?"

"Tell 'em, Murphy," Brooks snapped. "Tell them

about the little secret you've been keeping from all of us."

Mills, Hawk, and I all exchanged awkward looks.

Hawk wrinkled his nose. "How'd he find out?"

"You knew?" Brooks raged. "Both of you?"

Mills nodded once, and Hawk stood up straighter. "Brooks, it's Murphy. He's not a dirtbag. If it was anybody else, we would've told you."

I gave Hawk a short nod of thanks, grateful he was backing me up.

"Not a dirtbag? I'm sorry, how is he not a dirtbag? Murphy, how long have you been talking to my sister behind my back?"

"Since January," I replied.

Brooks nodded. "And not only did you keep your little phone relationship from me, but you freaking pretended to meet her for the first time this week. You two acted like strangers. Man, I don't even know what to say to you right now. You listened to me talk about how Cory ruined our friendship when he hurt my sister, and all the while you're talking to her behind my back?"

I swallowed. "If we could just talk about it—"

"Oh, now you wanna talk?" Brooks held up his hands. "Don't you think you should have talked to me about it the minute you met her on Connect? That way, I could have told you back then to stay the heck away from my sister."

"I'm sorry for lying to you. I am. Your friendship means a lot to me, man. You're like a brother to me." I took a hesitant step forward.

Brooks crossed his arms over his chest. "Nope. Screw that. There is no friendship. I'm not your brother. I'm done with all three of you lying sacks. In fact, I think I need to avoid having friends altogether. Man, I sure know how to pick 'em."

Hawk and Mills both shot me angry looks, and I knew I'd need to make amends with them for dragging them into this.

"Brooks, I love her. Okay? I know you're mad, I get it. I was wrong. And I'm sorry. But you're going to have to get on board. I love her."

Brooks let out a bitter laugh. "Oh, that changes things then, doesn't it? You love her? Bro. Get out. All three of you. We're done here."

19

IVY

"Thanks again for letting me stay here," I said, smiling at my sister-in-law.

I felt so at home in the two-bedroom townhouse she and Travis shared on base. I stayed there every time I visited them in San Diego; I even had a drawer of beach necessities and toiletries in their guest room.

"Anytime," Cat replied with a wink, handing me a cup of coffee across the kitchen island. She turned toward the living room and called to her friends, "Ellie, Liv, coffee's ready."

"Did you tell Travis I was staying here?" It had been four months since I'd last spoken to my brother. I'd tried—often—but he wouldn't have anything to do with me or Jake.

She shook her head. "No, but he's been super busy the last few days, so I've barely talked to him. He'll find out tonight when he gets home, though."

Ellie Hawkins and a very pregnant Olivia Mills came into the kitchen. They each grabbed a steaming mug of coffee and used the cream and sugar Cat had set out for them.

Olivia inhaled the aroma wafting from her cup. "Mmm. I seriously cherish my one sacred cup of coffee per day."

"I usually have two cups," Ellie said, taking a sip of hers. "Whenever I get pregnant, I'm going to have a hard time cutting it down to one."

"You could buy half-caf," Cat said with a shrug. "Then you can have two cups and it'll be the same amount of caffeine as one."

We all looked at each other with matching *Oh, smart* expressions.

"I'll probably check with my doctor whenever the time comes, just in case, but that sounds pretty legit. Have you given this a lot of thought or something?" Ellie asked Cat.

Cat shrugged. "Not gonna lie, we've talked about starting a family a lot more now that Liv's been pregnant. I'm getting baby fever."

I grinned. "Ah, I can't wait to be an auntie. That is, if my brother doesn't completely cut me out of his life."

The girls gave me sad looks, and Cat sighed. "I've tried to talk to him about it, Vee. He's so ..."

"Stubborn," I finished.

"Yeah," she agreed. "I figure once he's home it'll be different though. It's good you came out for the homecoming."

I picked at the edge of the countertop. "I'm here for Jake, though, really."

"Ivy ..." Ellie leaned forward onto the kitchen island, "Jake's a great guy. We've all known him for a while now, and he seriously has a heart of gold."

"I know," I said, not meeting her eyes. I had a feeling I knew where this was going.

"What Ellie's trying to say is," Olivia chimed in, "we care about him. The four of those guys are like a family, and we're like a family. But Travis is your blood. So, if Travis puts his foot down and can't get over the fact that you guys are together ... do you think you'd end things with Jake?"

"He's your brother," Ellie added quickly, holding up her hand. "We totally get how important that is. But we're also looking out for Jake, you know?"

It should have been an awkward conversation. I could tell they felt uncomfortable, but I got it. I was this unknown girl coming into their circle. But little did they know, I appreciated how they felt about Jake. I understood how much they cared about him. And I loved that he had a family like this, since I knew from spending so much time in the firehouse how important it was to have people willing to have your back.

"Jake is one of the good ones," I began. "I've talked to him every day for nearly his entire deployment, and as attracted as I am to him physically, it's his heart I've gotten to know the most. I promise, you guys have nothing to worry about with me hurting Jake. That's the last thing I want."

Cat gave me a small smile. "And what about your crazy brother?"

"He's going to have to get over it," I said, blowing out a breath. "We shouldn't have lied to him. I get that. He's right to be mad. But he can't stay mad forever."

The girls and I had finished our coffee and gotten ready for the homecoming together. Once we'd gotten all of the dramatic talk out of the way, we were just four women, anxiously awaiting the return of the men we loved. We stood together on the crowded flight line, chatting and taking pictures to pass the time.

In true Marine Corps fashion, the plane carrying the three hundred troops was delayed twice. Families stood anxiously in a barricaded area for hours, wondering when their loved ones would finally touch down.

"Another delay?" Olivia whined, checking her phone again. "My feet are killing me."

She looked adorable in her maternity dress and wedges, but after standing for this long, I was sure she was ready to fall over. "Let me go find you a chair."

"Here," a Marine in cammies materialized with a folding chair.

"Oh, bless you!" Olivia thanked the Marine, and gingerly sat down. She wasn't quite ready to pop, but it still looked pretty difficult to balance such a big bump on such a small frame.

Cat crossed her arms. "They can be as late as they want. I'm just glad to have a normal homecoming like this instead of what we went through last time."

Olivia and I shared a knowing look and I held up a hand. "Thank you, Jesus."

The last deployment these guys had been on had ended early for both Matt and Travis since they'd been shot, so they'd gone to hospitals instead of homecomings. At the time, being a firefighter's girlfriend and a Marine's sister meant I was no stranger to people I cared about being in dangerous professions, but I hadn't worried about Travis much before that day. It was one of the scariest times in my life. I shuddered at the memory, then made an effort to shake it off. This deployment hadn't been like that one. We were there to celebrate.

Military homecomings were a spectacular place to people-watch. Moms wrangled kids, doing all they could to keep their Americana outfits clean as they sat on the ground and played with small toys or tablets. Middle-aged folks bearing shirts emblazoned with Proud USMC Dad or Marine Mom stood in groups, gravitating together based on their age alone. There were several small groups of Marines who'd come home from the deployment early and were in attendance to make sure everything went smoothly with the main party.

And lastly, I enjoyed watching the photographers. They wore comfy clothes in neutral color palettes so they could move freely and not stand out. They watched the families who hired them and snapped photos of any picture-perfect moments, then faded into the background and scrolled their phone for a while so they weren't too intrusive while we waited out the delays. I knew they'd be ready when the time came, however, as I made eye contact with the local photographer I'd hired for the event.

Sure, I'd had a brief moment of panic thinking Jake would tease me for hiring a photographer, but honestly, it wasn't just his last deployment. We'd fallen in love while he traveled the world. I wanted to commemorate it. This deployment was the start of something I hoped to spend the rest of my life enjoying.

We'd spent the first couple of months sneaking conversations wherever we could fit them in. In Hawaii, we got to finally kiss and cuddle and act like a real couple—even if only at night on our private strolls along the beach. And once everything blew up with Travis, and we admitted we were in love, it only got more real from there. If Cat, Ellie, and Olivia all had their reasons for hiring photographers, that was mine.

My phone buzzed in my hand, jerking me back to reality. I couldn't help the grin that spread over my face, which of course, my photographer caught with her camera and then asked, "I assume they landed?"

I nodded, seeing that other family members were getting similar messages and cheering. The runway at Marine Corps Air Station Miramar was massive, and we were told they'd land near their hangars, unload some gear, and then the plane would taxi to the passenger terminal for the Marines to disembark.

"Should be any minute," my photographer said. "Here, hold your phone facing me so I can see the text from him. Great, smile big."

She snapped the picture and goose bumps radiated

up my arms. This was it. After months apart, after countless I love yous typed out or said through the phone, I was finally going to get my Marine back.

Of course, "any minute" turned into twenty minutes, because (again) Marine Corps. Thankfully, the time went by in a blur. I took photos with Cat and the other two girls, we watched the kids get straightened up by their moms, and people took their signs out and held them at the ready for when the plane came into view. The crowd buzzed with excitement when a few Marines wheeled the giant staircase forward in anticipation of unloading the passengers.

After what felt like forever, a large Boeing 737 came into view. An earsplitting cheer sounded from the crowd. This wasn't my first homecoming, since I'd gone to the one from Travis's first deployment several years ago. But it was my first deployment in love with one of the Marines coming home.

The perfectly timed sunset provided a pinkish glow over the runway and bounced off the white plane as it creeped along the runway and came to a stop before us. Another cheer sounded from the crowd when the door opened and they brought over the set of stairs. We all waved and yelled, staring at the open door, waiting for a sign of movement onboard. Finally, the first Marines began to disembark, sending the crowd into a frenzy.

There were waist-high cement barricades separating the families from the runway itself, and some Marines ran to greet their wives or girlfriends there instead of funneling into the opening. The Marines all wore their forest-green cammies and hats, so for a brief panicked moment, I worried I wouldn't be able to find Jake.

I wedged myself into a blank space at the barricade and squinted into the swarm of Marines jogging over from the plane. I felt the presence of my photographer nearby, knowing she was getting all the money shots of my anticipation.

As I scanned the faces of the smiling men and women rushing toward us, one Marine branched off from the rest and the movement caught my eye. It was Jake. He ran toward me, slipping off the giant green seabag that was strapped to his back. He dropped his seabag on my side of the barricade, placed a hand on top of it, and launched himself over and into my waiting arms.

My hands wrapped around the back of his neck as his arms tightened around my waist, lifting me off my feet. When our lips connected, the entire world faded away. The camera flashes in the fading sun, the cheering from other families, and all of the knots I'd been carrying around in my belly vanished into thin air. All I could register was the way my whole body relaxed into the familiar scent of him. Fresh, clean, light ... and yet, somehow, also rich and deep—like the ocean.

He set me on my feet and peppered me with quick kisses, a wide grin between each one. He took my hands and guided me out a few steps so he could look me up and down, his expression appreciative as he took in my dark-red blouse and black pants. His bright-blue eyes, the first thing I'd noticed about him, were happy and warm as they gave me a slow once-over.

"I missed you," he said, grabbing the back of my head and pulling me close, bringing his lips to my forehead.

"I missed you, too," I said, tucking my head under his chin and resting my cheek against the stiff fabric of his cammies. I looked up and saw the lens of a camera, unintentionally looking right into it. Well, that would be a good shot, I was sure.

"You got a homecoming photographer, huh?" He squeezed me and pulled back to look at my face. "You're like an official Marine girlfriend now."

I laughed. "You'll thank me for this when we're old, you know."

Jake brought his hands to the sides of my face like he had when we'd first met in Hawaii. His thumbs brushed over my face as he looked into my eyes, saying a lot without having to say anything at all. It occurred to me that we'd used a lot of words on this deployment to explain how we felt and build this deep connection. I wondered if we'd spend the next little while not talking, just being. As his lips closed over mine and my whole body warmed, I decided that was exactly what I wanted to happen.

20

JAKE

"Where do you want this?" Ivy asked, standing in the doorway of my new apartment holding a large box. I moved to grab for the box, but she took a step back. "I got it, I got it. Just tell me where to put it."

I chuckled. She was a strong, independent woman, and if I didn't stop trying to help her carry things, she'd likely wind up throwing something at me. "What does it say?"

She read the writing on the top of the box. "'USMC.' That's kinda vague."

"It's all of my awards and other moto stuff. Will you put it in there?" I pointed to the den.

"What's 'moto'?" she asked as she walked through the open French doors of the den and placed the box on the floor.

"It's short for motivated. It's like ..." I pumped my fist sarcastically, "oorah. You know?"

She giggled. "Gotcha."

"Thank you for your help today."

"Of course," she said, kissing me on the cheek. "I'm happy this day is finally here."

I gazed around the apartment and took in my new space. I had to admit, it was impressive. As a single Marine, I'd lived in the barracks for the last eight years, so really any apartment would have been an improvement. But my new government contractor salary was three times that of my active duty pay, so when Ivy offered to help me find an apartment, I'd told her my budget and instructed her to go big.

My new place had a large living area between two full bedrooms. The den was off the dining room and I planned to turn it into a home gym. The kitchen was large and open, with a breakfast bar that had enough room for a few barstools. There was a balcony off the living room that overlooked the pool area, which is what had sold me on the place.

The apartment complex was what Ivy referred to as "resort style," so the pool area had super fancy barbecue spaces, fire pits, cabanas, a zero entry pool, and even a lazy river. There was a game room off the lobby with pool tables and a few dart boards, and a small movie theatre off to the side. I wasn't sure if I'd ever utilize those rooms for a party or anything, since I didn't have any friends in town, but maybe someday.

That being said, before I could even think about hosting anyone at my new apartment, I needed to get some furniture. It had only taken us a few minutes to bring in the few boxes of stuff I'd had at the barracks, and other than my flat-screen and game console sitting on the floor in my living room, that's all I owned.

I scratched my head. "I'm about to say something dangerous."

"Ooh, please do." Ivy wagged her eyebrows at me.

"Wanna go shopping?"

"What do I need so many shelves for?" I asked, tilting my head at the large entertainment center. It had space in the middle for my TV to hang with a cabinet underneath for the consoles, games, and controllers. That right there would have been enough for me, but there was way more to it than that. On each side were two large bookshelves that were connected at the top by a row of square cubbyholes.

"Books," Ivy said with a shrug, "and, I dunno, you can display all of that Marine Corps stuff here."

I wrinkled my nose. "A lot of guys make a moto wall

with their Marine Corps stuff when they get out. I figured I'd put mine in the den with the gym, not around my TV."

"That makes sense."

I put my hands on my hips and looked around the massive furniture store. "This is a trip."

"What?" She took one of my hands in hers.

"Furniture shopping."

"What about it?"

I took a deep breath. "The barracks have furniture. I've never had to furnish my own place before. It's just ... after growing up the way I did ... it's just cool to think about how far I've come. That I have this great job and military service behind me. I'm picking out nice stuff to put in my own place. It's cool."

Ivy gave my hand a squeeze. "I'm really happy for you, Jake."

"Anyway," I said, clearing my throat and gesturing back to the entertainment center she'd suggested. "I don't have enough books for all these shelves. I was hoping for something a little more ..."

"Simple?"

I nodded. "Yes."

"Let's keep looking." She took my hand and led me to another area of the furniture store. "You know ... I happen to have a lot of books, if you decide you want them to move in with you someday."

I raised my brow at her. "Oh, do you?"

"I sure do. I bet they would make good roommates. You know, since they're already used to living with other people." She batted her eyes at me. "They know how to keep to themselves, they don't leave their stuff all over the common areas, and they're super cute to look at. You might enjoy having them around more often."

I couldn't help the laugh that escaped me as I squeezed her hand. "And these books ... wouldn't their other roommates miss them and come hunt me down for taking them away?"

She bit her lip, considering this. "I think they'd understand."

"That's good," I said, pulling her into my arms and kissing her softly. "Would you really want to move in with me?"

She blushed and stepped away, taking my hand again as we strolled through the rows of living room furniture on display. "Probably not yet ... but I can't help but think about it with all this furniture shopping."

"Well," I said, leaving her to throw myself onto a nearby sectional, "feel free to help me furnish this place to your liking. Just in case."

She joined me on the sofa, stretching out on the chaise lounge and closing her eyes. "Ooh, this one's nice."

"Agreed."

"If I help you pick out all the furniture, what happens if we break up and you hate the stuff I picked?"

I shrugged. "I'll probably take it out in the desert and shoot it or something. Isn't that what you Texas people would do?"

She picked up a throw pillow and tossed it at me. "Dumb."

"Can I help you folks with anything?" a stern-looking woman asked, her arms crossed in disapproval over our brief pillow fight.

I sobered and cleared my throat. "Honey, pull out our list. Time to get serious."

"Yes, sir," she said, saluting.

I face-palmed. "Don't do that."

21

IVY

"Mom," I called out the back door. "Where are the sparklers we bought last weekend?"

My mom looked up from the centerpiece she was arranging on one of the five round tables in our backyard. "Look in the guest room. I think I stashed them in there because the garage was too hot."

I ducked back into the kitchen and pointed down the hall. "Guest room, first door on the left."

"On it," Rachel replied, heading off to get them.

Nora, Rachel, and I had been at my parents' house all morning helping them set up for their annual barbeque for Labor Day weekend. It was a big event for them and there were usually about a hundred people in attendance.

My dad invited all of the people who worked for him and his friends from their country club. My mom's guests were all of her hobby club ladies. There was book club, knitting club, murder mystery club, women's golf—you name the hobby, she had a weekly meeting for it.

My brother always invited his friends, whose parents were friends with our parents anyway, and I invited mine. It was the one and only social event we hosted without fail each year, and the only difference this time was that my brother wouldn't be there.

Jake: Is this a pool party?

Me: Yes.

Jake: Cool. Do you need any help setting up? I can come early.

I was about to text him and tell him to come on over when the front door opened and in walked Travis and Cat. My jaw dropped, and I put my phone on the counter, forgetting all about texting Jake back.

"You said you weren't coming." I couldn't help the smile that reflexively spread across my face. He might be mad at me, but I still loved my brother and hated these months of conflict.

He grunted. "Blame this one."

"What can I say?" Cat said with a sly grin. "I haven't missed this party in almost a decade. I wasn't about to start now."

"Does Mom know?" I asked, crossing my arms so I wouldn't hug Travis like I had at the homecoming. He'd given me a one-armed pat on the back. It was the lightest touch, as if he were hugging a smelly stranger, and it had seriously bruised my ego.

Travis shook his head. "Nope. Cat wanted it to be a surprise."

"Oh my ..." Our mom gasped when she came in the back door and saw her son and daughter-in-law standing in the living room. She opened the back door again, yelled for our dad, then practically ran to her son, and wrapped him in a huge mom-hug. "My sweetheart. Thank you so much for coming. You have no idea how much it broke my heart that you wouldn't be here."

"I know, I'm sorry, Mama." Travis glared at me over Mom's shoulder, then closed his eyes and hugged her back.

My parents hadn't gone to the homecoming because they figured they'd see him at the barbeque, but after our awkwardness that night, he'd called my mom and said he wasn't ready to have quality family time with me yet.

"Oh, thank the good Lord. And you," Mom said, moving to put a hand on Cat's cheek and hugging her, too, "I'm sure you had something to do with this, so thank you."

"Well, look what the cat dragged in," Dad boomed

as he came in from the backyard. "Nice of you to join us, Trav. You had your mother in tears, you know."

Travis had the decency to look guilty, then cut me a sideways glance. I stuck my tongue out at him. Yes, I understood what I'd done was wrong. But he was also a huge pain in my rear, and it was his fault I'd been too scared to tell him about Jake in the first place.

Mom looked between us and held up a finger. "You know what? This ends here. Now that I've got both of my babies under one roof, it's time for me to speak my mind."

Cat cringed and tiptoed over to my dad, and the two of them inched away from us and toward the kitchen. I shot them a dirty look as they passed. Cowards.

"Now," Mom continued, her Southern accent thickening like it always did when she got worked up. "Ivy Grace. You should not have hidden this from your brother."

"I know, Mama," I said.

"Let me finish," she scolded me. "I know you and I have already made amends for your sneaking around with Jake behind our backs in Hawaii. But that's us. You still owe Travis an apology. It makes sense he'd be worried about losing another friend if things went south."

"I've tried," I defended myself. "But this jerk has a

thick skull and tends to ignore people who attempt to apologize to him. Ask Cory."

Travis rolled his eyes and crossed his arms across his chest, stubborn as a brick wall.

"Travis Michael," our mom turned on him. "Have you been ignoring Ivy's attempts to make up with you?"

My brother looked down.

"Is that what I taught you?" she asked. "Is that how we do things in this house when we fight?"

Travis wrinkled his nose. "Mama, we're not two kids fighting over toys. We're too grown for you to make us both squeeze into one of Daddy's shirts for five minutes. This is bigger than that, okay? She knew how upset I'd be if she dated another one of my friends. I lost my best friend when she lost her boyfriend last time, and now she wants to take another one away? That doesn't sit right with me."

I bit my lip. He was my big brother. When we were kids and we'd fight, our mom would slip one of my dad's oversize T-shirts over both of our heads and we'd have to stay stuck together like that for five minutes.

Depending on the severity of the fight, sometimes we'd end up laughing until we fell down only one minute into it. Other times, it would take the full five minutes, but the end result was the same. We were best friends growing up, and we never stayed mad for long.

But he was right. This time was different. I'd lied to

him because I'd known it would hurt him if I told him what I was doing. And that had hurt him worse.

My mom looked at me. "Ivy, he said his piece. You say yours."

"Trav," I said, eyes welling up with tears. "I'm sorry. I didn't mean to hurt you. I shouldn't have lied about Jake."

"You shouldn't have ever started talking to Jake," he cut in.

I shook my head. "I won't apologize for that. If I could go back and do anything differently, it would be that I wouldn't have kept it from you. I would have told you as soon as I figured out who he was. But I wouldn't have stopped talking to him."

Travis crossed his arms over his chest. "That's ridiculous. Why him?"

"You know exactly why," I said, holding out my arms in frustration. "If anyone does, you do. You know what a good guy he is. And if you could see past your anger over this whole thing, you'd admit that he's perfect for me and you'd be happy we found each other."

My brother's eyes softened around the edges, and hope took root in my belly.

"It looks like y'all are making some progress here," Mom said quietly, backing out of the room. "Now, pretend this room is one of Daddy's shirts. Don't leave until you're laughing. You hear?"

"Thanks, Mama," I said, giving her a small smile as she left before turning back to my brother. "Trav, listen. I talked to Cory the other day. We talked all about how we weren't meant to be and it was probably best that he left when he did. There's no hard feelings between us, and we're able to go back to being friends."

He snorted. "Good for you two."

"I know you guys will have to figure out your own problems. I can't speak for why he left without saying anything to you. Maybe he was scared you'd try to talk him out of it or be mad at him for hurting me. I honestly don't know. But either way, there's no reason why you two can't work it out and be friends again. If I can forgive him for leaving me when I thought he was going to propose, you can forgive him for the stuff on your end."

"What, so you're saying that if me, you, and Cory can go back to singing "Kumbaya" after all this crap, I should be able to do the same thing when you and Jake break up? Ivy, c'mon. Why should I have to keep having problems with my friends just because you decide to date them?"

I lunged forward and pushed his solid chest, and of course, he didn't move an inch. "Do you hear yourself? You're acting like I'm some hussy making the rounds through your friends. Is that what you think of me?"

Travis's nostrils flared. "Of course not."

"Then knock it off," I said through my teeth. "Cory and I were together our whole freaking lives. We grew up and went our separate ways. I'm sorry you got caught in the crossfire, but me being a grown woman and falling in love with Jake isn't the same thing at all. And did it ever occur to you that maybe I fall for your friends because you're my big brother and I look up to you? Maybe I figure if these guys are good enough to be friends with you, then they're good enough for me?"

His brows shot up to his hairline and he pursed his lips. "Well, shoot."

"Right? I bet you feel bad now, huh?" I asked, a ragged laugh escaping me.

"I kinda do, actually. Dang." He cracked a smile and stared at me for a long moment.

"Well?"

Right when I was about to start hollering again, my big brother wrapped one of his huge arms around me, pulling me tight against his chest. "I'm sorry, Vee. I wasn't thinking about any of this ... well, like you were."

"That's 'cause you're a stubborn donkey butt and always have been," I said into his shirt.

He pulled back and held me at arm's length, hands on my shoulders. "Where's your boyfriend? I figure I have to go kiss and make up with him now, too."

"I'm not telling if you're gonna kiss him. He's mine."

With a quick flick of his wrist, Travis had me in a

playful headlock, rubbing his fist against the top of my head. I struggled hard against him, yelling about my hair and calling for our mom. She poked her head in the door, smiling. "See? That T-shirt trick works every time."

EPILOGUE

IVY

"Okay, guys!" I clapped my hands to get my students' attention. "Go sit at the tables marked with your color."

The kids, each wearing their assigned color from head to toe, scurried to the tables designated with their color. We'd been working on a colorful theme all week. There was only one week until winter break, and we'd just gotten back in the swing of things from Thanksgiving break, so it was a crazy time of the year.

Rainbow Day had been something they'd been looking forward to since they first heard about it, but I had to admit, I was a little sad our colorful lesson was coming to a close. I'd spent so many late nights crafting and putting together all of the vibrant projects. Jake would either come to the bungalow and help me work on them there or I'd bring all of my stuff to his apartment. He had turned into quite the skilled teacher's assistant in the months he'd been living in Fort Worth. He could cut out gingerbread men with the best of them.

I thought back to the last night we'd worked on red-colored projects at his apartment. He'd made me spaghetti with meat sauce and grabbed a bottle of red wine. We'd joked about how we didn't like it much but it fit the theme. He'd even ordered my favorite red velvet Bundt cake from the bakery I only went to for special occasions. His eyes had sparkled as he'd fed me a bite of the cake and told me that I should throw that rule away. It could be a special occasion any time we wanted it to be. And I'd melted, obviously.

"Vee?" Nora popped her head into my classroom. "Special delivery."

Before I had a chance to react, she opened the door and wheeled in a cart with several vases of roses on it. Each vase held a dozen roses in a different color. Rachel was behind her with another cart. My heart squeezed and I watched in awe as they took the vases, one by one, and placed them at the center of their coordinating table.

My students were so excited and went on and on about how pretty they were. Part of me was processing the romantic gesture, but the bigger part—the part that was in kindergarten teacher mode—was telling my kids not to touch the roses. Yes, it's real glass. Yes, there's water in it, please don't make it spill. No, we don't want to touch the petals. Just look with our eyes.

Rachel and Nora finished distributing the vases and came over to me, the mist in their eyes enough to warn me that this charade wasn't over yet. They each hugged me briefly and left and I shook my hands to try to calm my nerves. What was Jake up to? Was it what I thought it was? Or was I reading too much into this and would have yet another embarrassing moment, waiting for a proposal that wouldn't come?

Before I could fall too far down the rabbit hole of self-doubt, the classroom door opened again. This time, it was the front office secretary. "You have a visitor, Ms. Brooks."

My heart tumbled around inside my chest as I waited anxiously to see his face.

"Thank you, Mrs. Thompson," I said with a smile for the older woman as she opened the door wider to let him in.

Jake entered the room with a big smile and strong, decisive steps. There was nothing about his expression or his body language that suggested he was nervous. He wore my favorite dark jeans and the charcoal-and-black Aloha shirt he'd been wearing the night we'd first met. It hung open over a black T-shirt that fit tightly across his broad chest. In my natural reaction of looking him up and down, I tilted my head in surprise as I noticed the flip-flops on his feet. The shirt itself was out of place in Texas, not to mention in December, but the flip-flops were too much.

"Jake, what are you wearing?" I asked through a laugh, my shaky hand moving up to cover my mouth.

He held his arms out and looked down. "What, this old thing? I thought you liked this shirt."

"I do, you just look like you're ready for the beach." I gestured around my classroom decorated for the winter holidays. "It's almost Christmas."

"That's right," he said, and then turned to my students, who were starting to get rambunctious. "And class, where is the absolute best place to spend Christmas?"

All at once, twenty-five little voices shouted out different answers.

"My mom's house!"

"Grandma's house!"

Various other states were named by the military kids who had out-of-state families.

One kid yelled, "The movie theatre!"

Another said, "I'm Jewish."

Jake and I looked at each other and laughed as we tried to take in the different answers and acknowledge them all.

"Those are great places," Jake told my class when I'd

gotten them to settle down. "But guess where Ms. Brooks is going to spend Christmas?"

Again, because five-year-olds don't do rhetorical questions, they all shouted out their guesses.

I heard a few of my sharper kids yell things like, "The beach!" or "Hawaii."

Jake pointed to them and said, "Yes!"

I covered the sides of my face with my hands as he pulled two plane tickets out of his pocket and handed them to me. I took the tickets, seeing our names on two first-class tickets back to Oahu. I looked up at him, a huge grin on my face. "Christmas in Hawaii?"

"Before you say yes to that, we have to finish Rainbow Day. Right, guys?"

The class cheered in response.

"Okay, let's get started," Jake addressed the class. He didn't introduce himself since they'd met him at the carnival, book fair, family game night, or some other school-sponsored event he'd volunteered at with me. "Red table, since you're the first color of the rainbow, let's start with you. Can you there, with the red cowboy hat—yep, you—can you carefully take one of your red roses out and bring it to Ms. Brooks?"

Thomas did as he was asked, and I thanked him.

"The red rose," Jake said, acting like a quintessential kindergarten teacher, "signifies love, honesty, and bravery."

I swallowed through the lump in my throat as he took my hand and spoke lower to me than he had to the class.

"Ivy, I obviously love you, but you also make me brave. I'm not sure if I would have stood up to your brother for anyone else."

I couldn't hold back the laugh that bubbled up as I watched him turn back to the kids.

"All right, orange table, you're up. You with the orange sunglasses, will you bring a rose to Ms. Brooks, please?"

Sara brought me my rose and hugged me tightly around the waist before sitting back down.

"The orange rose is for energy and excitement." Again, he said that part for the class and then turned to me. "I'm so excited to spend the rest of my life with you, Ivy."

I let out a breath and looked up at the ceiling, willing my eyes to stop watering. There were several more colors to get through, and I would be a mess at the end of this if I started crying now.

"Yellow! You with the yellow feather thing, yeah, you. Will you bring Ms. Brooks the next rose, please?"

I took the yellow rose and hug from Caitlin, then waited for the next meaning from Jake.

"The yellow rose stands for friendship. Who here has a friend that is very special to them?"

I covered my mouth with my hand again as I watched him interact with my students. They called out the names of their friends and hugged each other, running to other tables and almost giving me a heart attack for fear they would knock over the vases. I helped Jake quiet them down again when he looked at me with an adorable *oops, they're crazy* kind of expression.

"I'm grateful for our friendship," Jake said to me, squeezing my hand, "but also that we were able to fix everything with your brother. Because that's an important friendship for both of us."

I squeezed his hand in return before he let go to move on with the class.

"What's the next color?" he asked the class and nodded when they yelled their answer. "Yes, green. Okay, green table, you with the … green mohawk. That's awesome, man. You bring the next flower."

Steven brought me my flower, but unlike his crazy hair would suggest, he got awkward when he was the center of attention. He quickly handed it to me, then ran away.

"Green roses are for hope," Jake said. "As in, I hope I don't fall on my face in front of all of these kids because that would be embarrassing!"

The class roared with laughter, and I was grateful for the comic relief in the middle of all the sweetness.

That was my Jake, though. He was kind and serious, but made me laugh every day.

"Blue table," Jake pointed to the table in the back corner. "How about you with the blue dress. Will you bring up a blue flower for your teacher?"

Tinsley skipped to the front, handed me the flower, and motioned for me to bend down so she could tell me a secret. I leaned close and felt her warm breath on my ear as she whispered, "Does this guy love you or something?"

I nodded and patted her on the shoulder. "He sure does."

"Blue roses are for new opportunities," Jake said. He turned to me. "I'm so grateful for the opportunity that brought me here to Fort Worth and to you."

"Me too," I said, heat warming my cheeks.

"Last color, guys, here we go," Jake said, clapping his hands once and rubbing them together. "Purple table. Guy in the purple dinosaur costume. Is that Barney? You don't know who Barney is?" He wrinkled his nose at me. "What are you teaching these kids? Anyway, bring up the flower, Barney."

Joey barreled to the front of the room and handed me the flower, then did a crazy disco dance for the class while Jake came over and touched my cheek. "Purple is for love at first sight. And I will never forget that day when I was scrolling through all the pretty girls in Texas, and then I found you."

I snorted. "I stopped the scroll?"

"So fast."

We both laughed, and when he glanced down at my lips and it looked like he was about to kiss me, I shook my head backed up an inch or two.

Jake turned back to the class. "Okay, guys. That's it. And do you know what Ms. Brooks has in her hands now?"

Several students yelled out things like, "A rainbow!" or "All of the colors!"

Jake nodded his head. "You're right, she has all of the colors. And do you know what a bouquet of all of the colors means?"

My kids called out random guesses, their voices turning to white noise as the classroom faded away. All I could see was Jake, reaching into his pocket and pulling out a small box, then dropping down to one knee.

Nora and Rachel squealed from the doorway. They, and a few of my other teacher friends, had probably been standing there the entire time. I saw that Nora had her phone out, and I knew I'd be grateful for that video for years to come.

"Ivy Brooks," Jake said, opening the box to reveal the most gorgeous ring I'd ever seen. It was round with a halo of diamonds and a white gold band that was also covered in small diamonds.

"Yes?" I blinked my watery eyes and focused them back on his beautiful blue ones as he continued.

"A bouquet of all the colors means that you are my everything. You mean everything to me, and I thank God for you every day. Will you marry me?"

I didn't even have to think about it. "Yes."

He stood and pulled me into his arms, swinging me around and planting a huge kiss on my lips. My colleagues at the door and the kids in the class were all cheering around us, and I couldn't believe this moment was real.

Jake lowered me to my feet and pulled the ring out of the box, placing it on my finger, both of us laughing at how much my hand shook.

"Back to Christmas in Hawaii," Jake said. "I was thinking maybe ... a beach wedding?"

"Already?"

"Why not?"

I considered this. After many deep conversations, Jake knew all about my history with Cory and the big country wedding we'd talked about having. Jake also knew my heart hadn't really been in it, but it was what we'd always talked about doing, so that was the plan.

The idea of eloping to Hawaii—a place very near and dear to us—was exactly the kind of wedding I wanted. No big crowd, no big expectations, and no stressful planning. And since I knew without a doubt that I was ready to be his wife, there was no real reason to delay it.

"I'm in." I grinned at him, excitement coursing through me.

Jake wagged his eyebrows at me and then noticed something over my head. "You're going to have to change your name up there to 'Mrs. Murphy' when you come back from Christmas break."

I raised my arms around his neck, my new ring on my left hand and my flowers still clutched in my right. "I can't wait."

If you haven't read it yet, you can get a free digital copy of the prequel to this series just for signing up for my newsletter!

Visit the link below to read Vince & Sara's story:

http://www.jessmastorakos.com/forever-with-you

*As for the **next book in the series**, it's time for Brooks and Cat to get their story.*

Learn more at the link below:

http://www.jessmastorakos.com/memories-of-you

Made in the USA
Monee, IL
14 June 2020

33662005R10146